RATTLER

RATTLER

by

John Dyson

Dales Large Print Books
Long Preston, North Yorkshire,
BD23 4ND, England.

British Library Cataloguing in Publication Data.

Dyson, John
    Rattler.

A catalogue record of this book is
available from the British Library

ISBN   1-84262-120-3 pbk

First published in Great Britain 2000 by Robert Hale Limited

Cover illustration © Ballestar by arrangement with
Norma Editorial S.A.

The right of John Dyson to be identified as the author of this
work has been asserted by him in accordance with the
Copyright, Designs and Patents Act, 1988

Published in Large Print 2001 by arrangement with
Robert Hale Limited

Dales Large Print is an imprint of Library Magna Books Ltd.

Printed and bound in Great Britain by
T.J. (International) Ltd., Cornwall, PL28 8RW

One

Johnny Rattler climbed up stealthily through the Spanish bayonet, yucca and cacti. Every damn thing in this country had hooks and barbs trying to tear a man's flesh or clothing to shreds. The boulders were hot as hell and as sharp as razors. The sun beat down, and in this airless gully it was like being inside a bakehouse. Sweat trickled from beneath his wide-brimmed hat, down over his cheek, jawbone and strong-muscled neck to his chest beneath the wool army jacket with its sergeant's chevrons. At nineteen he was young to be a sergeant of scouts, but men grew up fast in these parts and he knew the Apache tricks, knew their lingo. He knew Kothluni and his boys were somewhere about. He could smell them. And he knew that any moment one of the savages might

7

leap from behind these rocks. He licked his dry lips and headed on up to the ridge.

'What's he doing?' Lieutenant Giles Prendergast asked. He sat his horse half a mile away and through his glass watched Rattler snake – like the reptile after which he was named – over the rim of the ridge. 'Looks like he's seen something, sor,' his sergeant of cavalry growled.

Sergeant McMullan was a barrel of a man. His forage cap perched on his bald head, his coarse features reddened by whiskey. There was no love lost between James McMullan and his sergeant of scouts, Johnny Rattler, but he had a canny respect for his abilities. 'He knows what he's doing.'

Young Prendergast was fresh out on the frontier from West Point and his uniform was unsullied by thorn or storm, unfaded yet by sun, unlike those of the thirty troopers who rested their mounts around him. Months out on the trail had left them with uncut hair and beards, their uniforms muddied and torn. As for the scouts, the lieutenant had never seen such an evil-looking bunch, more like a gang of desperadoes.

'Shouldn't he give us some signal?'

'Hold your horses, sor. We don't want to ride into an ambush.'

Rattler had, indeed, seen something. This border country between Arizona and Mexico was as yet barely mapped or explored, its vast *barrancas* known only to *bandidos*, Indians, *comancheros*, or gringo smugglers. There were a few frontier scum who blithely braved its dangers for reward and one of them was rattling along a narrow trail that weaved through the rocky canyons: Tribollet!

Jacques Tribollet, in his silk plug hat and frock coat, sat on the box of his wagon and lashed his four mules forward. The contraption was as gaudy as a fairground caravan, its sides garishly enscrolled, 'Tribollet's Travelling Saloon'. He was a whiskey dealer and he didn't care who knew it, or who he sold it to. Tribollet had lived a

9

strange life. Born when an Austrian archduke was emperor of Mexico (for the brief period before he was put up before a firing squad), the spawn of a French soldier and Yaqui Indian woman, he had grown up as part of the flotsam of the frontier, living by his wits. He had aspired to be a saloon-keeper for he had noticed that, like the piano-player, they rarely got shot. They were too useful. All he had to show for his efforts were a hole-in-the-wall joint in Tucson, and this wagon, which he otherwise used to hawk a bunch of jaded whores and his roulette wheels around the far-flung *ranchos*.

'That bastard,' Rattler hissed, a cold hatred seething in him. This was not because on this occasion Tribollet was without any doubt taking a consignment of cheap whiskey out to Kothluni and his warriors, but because he was Rattler's natural father. Tribollet had mated with Rattler's American mother, kept her as one of his girls, used her and abused her, and kicked them both out when he was tired of them.

Johnny Rattler frowned, raised his Springfield carbine to his shoulder and waited until Tribollet was a few hundred yards away below. He knew he was breaking the rules. The crack of the carbine echoing through the canyons would be heard miles away, warning anyone in the vicinity. He squeezed the trigger and sent his father's silk hat flying. He would have liked to have blown his head from his shoulders.

'Nom de Dieu!' Tribollet hauled back the mules and the contraption creaked to a halt. He fastened the reins, looked back quickly for his hat, and up at the ridge. He reached tentatively for his rifle. Another shot cracked out, a bullet whined, hit the rifle stock and sent it spinning into the dust. 'Holy Shit!' Tribollet stared at his blood-streaked knuckles.

Lt Prendergast was trying to hold his startled horse as he saw Rattler go leaping over the ridge. 'What the devil's he playing at?'

'Looks like the young idjit's attackin'

single-handed,' McMullan roared. 'We better go after him, boys.'

Johnny Rattler went ploughing down on foot through a debris of dirt and rocks, giving wild screams like an attacking savage. Tribollet raised his arms to the heavens with alarm. But when he recognized his son he swore foully and for a full three minutes. 'Look what you done to my hand!'

'That ain't nothing to what I'd like to have done.' The lithe and handsome young scout stood covering him with his Springfield. 'That's only a crease. You deserve a slug through your evil heart for the way you treated us.'

'What you talkin' 'bout?'

'You know what I'm talking about. You kicked my mother and me out to fend for ourselves. You wouldn't help her when she was sick and came begging you.'

'Aw, is that all that's worryin' you? You don't understand, these thangs happen 'tween man and woman. She was a fine-lookin' gal. I wonder what the hell happened to her?'

'You know what happened to her. The 'pache got her on that stage we was on. She ain't been seen or heard of since.'

It was a strange conversation to be having, the first real conversation he had ever had with Tribollet. They had seen each other about from time to time in the frontier towns but his father had always pretended not to know him.

'You got your mother's looks when she was young,' Tribollet wheedled, attempting friendship. 'But that crow-black hair of yourn's more like your Yaqui grandmother's.' He sucked at his knuckles and spat blood. 'I heard tell you'd become quite a shootist. Some shot that was. There ain't many men can shoot like that.'

Rattler wiped a trickle of sweat from his bare bronzed chest and grinned, scornfully. It was the first time his father had recognized him as a man or given a grudging compliment. 'Yeah, I could have easily killed you.'

13

He went around the back, poked through the canvas with his carbine, broke the top off a wooden case and pulled out a bottle of White Lightning. He jerked the cork with his teeth, took a mouthful, gargled and spat it out. 'The real McCoy!'

Tribollet jumped down to retrieve his hat, studying the bullet hole. 'What the hell you doing? That's private property.'

Father and son eyed each other frankly and fully for the first time in a decade, not without a certain curiosity. 'You still up to your old tricks? Selling poison to the 'pache.'

Tribollet had traces of Gallic handsomeness, but his face was bloated by too much of his own booze, lined hard by greed and selfishness. His hair was thick and black like his son's, but streaked with grey. 'Apache ain't my enemy,' he said. 'I ain't no gringo. Kothluni wants what I got. Me and him' – he crossed the fingers on his unscathed hand – 'we're like this.'

Rattler wondered what Kothluni would

pay him with: stolen gold, guns, or slaves, girls snatched from some Mexican village, whom his father would sell to the saloons or maybe put to work himself?

'What gives you the right to come shooting at me? What you doin' out here, anyhow?'

As Lieutenant Prendergast at the head of his outfit of scouts and cavalry came over the ridge, and they picked their way down, Tribollet cursed some more in French.

When the troopers saw the bottle in Rattler's hand they whooped with glee, clambered from their mounts and began looting Tribollet's wagon, pushing him to one side, ignoring his protests.

'Hold it, boys,' Sergeant McMullan roared. 'One mouthful each. That's all you're allowed in this heat. You can put a bottle in your saddle-bag. We'll do our partying when we get back.'

'If we get back,' one of the troopers said, taking a second throatful. McMullan smashed the bottle from his hand.

'What are you doing?' the lieutenant demanded in his Boston tones. 'Who is this man?'

Tribollet was frantically trying to take note with pencil and paper how much was being looted. 'That's forty bottles at five dollars a bottle. I'm holding you responsible for this, Lieutenant. I'll be putting my bill in.'

'Shut up.' McMullan cuffed him a back-hander across the face, and started batting out at his men, too. 'Get back on your damn horses. Let's have some battle readiness. That fool shootin' musta roused every 'pache in twenty miles.'

'Sergeant, I asked you a question.' Prendergast was trying hard to remain calm. 'What's going on?'

'He's a lowdown whiskey trader,' Mc-Mullan said, and added with deep sarcasm, 'Sor.'

'What do you mean? Who is there out here to sell it to?'

'Who d'ye think, man? The Apaches. This load would really git 'em riled up. This is

Jacques Tribollet, the lowest of the low. He oughta be strung up.'

'Lieutenant, I am an honest trader,' Tribollet began but McMullan cuffed him again.

'You.' Prendergast haughtily addressed Rattler. 'What did you mean by firing those shots?'

Rattler flashed a grin at his scouts. Some were full-blooded Apaches, squatted around, sullen-faced with long hair and red headbands, blue coats. Others were white men, in beards and greasy buckskins, pan-handlers down on their luck, who had taken the job for the ten dollars a month pay, plus keep.

'I wanted to put a scare in him,' Rattler said.

'Don't you realize you've given away our position to the enemy? Are you mad?'

'Ar, don't wet yourself, Lieutenant. I got an idea.'

The men sniggered at his cocky attitude to their superior. Their opinion of Prendergast was not much higher than Rattler's. Prendergast bristled, colour rising to his pale cheeks. 'Watch the way you speak to me. I could take your stripes for this.'

'Ar, get off your high horse, Lieutenant. You wanna hear my idea, or not?'

'Sergeant McMullan, I will not permit looting. All of those bottles must be returned to this man. We will take his wagon into protective custody.'

McMullan sighed. 'Let's hear the kid's idea, shall we?'

Johnny Rattler jerked his head for the lieutenant to join him on the ground, and walked away a few paces. Prendergast frowned as fiercely as his baby-faced features permitted and stepped down.

'Look,' Rattler said, in a low intense voice, 'this whiskey's been promised to Kothluni. Why don't we offer it to him?'

'You *are* crazy. I thought so.'

'Look!' Rattler caught the young officer by his tunic before he walked away. 'It's the perfect bait for an ambush. All we gotta do is take up positions in the rocks along this ravine and wait for Kothluni to come to us. We can smash one of the wagon wheels so it looks like a breakdown. We can leave Tribollet at the wagon. He can say he fired to bring them to him. He can sell 'em the whiskey and get out of it on one of the mules to take his chances. We can attack as soon as he's clear, or wait a few minutes until they've all gotten drunk. How about that?'

Prendergast studied the dark-eyed young sergeant and shook his head. 'I don't like it.'

'It's worth a try,' McMullan drawled. 'Sor … would save us a hell of a lot of galloping about the countryside and maybe running into a trap of theirs. All we gotta do is leave the horses the far side of the ridge and dig in here. There's plenty of cover.'

Lt Prendergast stroked his close-shaven chin, as if in deep thought. 'Very well,' he said. 'Give the orders.'

The waiting was the hard part. Especially in

this 120-degree heat, with all the flies buzzing round. Perspiration dripped from McMullan's nose as time crawled. Maybe Kothluni was too cautious? Maybe he would send men along the ridge and see the horses? He was a renegade chief who had been raiding for a long time and a thousand soldiers in the field had never caught him. 'Tell that soldier along there to keep his carbine down,' McMullan growled, cramped behind his rock.

Rattler peered through the yucca leaves at his father slumped despondently on the box of the wagon, supping a bottle of his own whiskey. Occasionally he would break into some maundering French song to keep his spirits up. They had told him in no uncertain terms that they would kill him if he gave a hint of the game away, or refused to co-operate. Rattler gave a scoffing grin, and touched, for luck, the diamondback's rattle hanging from a thong around his neck. He didn't give a damn, he thought, if Tribollet got killed. Bitterly, he remembered the few times he had visited his father's saloon in Tucson. It was just some lowdown adobe hole in the wall. Yes, his mother had taken him there once begging him to help them. He could not forget how Tribollet had kicked them out into the street.

He waited through the long hot afternoon and it all came back to him. His mother, an American girl, who had become a 'dance hostess' after her parents were killed in a fire, had lost her job. She was ill and weak, probably through some botched abortion. She had decided to take the stage with her nine-year-old son to try to look up relatives in San Diego. They had been twenty miles out of Tucson when the Apache struck, shooting down the lead horses. The driver and adult male passengers had little chance and were all killed and mutilated. His mother and another woman had been raped before his eyes by the warriors, and dragged away, screaming, thrown over horses. Johnny Rattler had not seen her again. She had probably been sold into slavery over the border to work in the mines, or to some *federale* chief to spend her days as a prized white-skinned concubine. Or else, she was a squaw. Or she was dead.

Johnny, himself, had been abducted by the Apaches and taken to live in their camp in a cave high above Hell Canyon. They had often watched the soldiers trickling along below searching for them. He had soon become acclimatized to their ways, could shoot a bow, roast mescal, ride a pony like the best of them. They had been kindly enough to him in their savage way. In time 'Rattler' was going out on horse-raiding expeditions with them. It was his job to sneak up to some settlement, rattle his snake-tail rattle and scare the settlers' horses out of the corral. That was how some Apaches gave him his name, a name he kept in later life. In some ways those had been exciting days, but one thing he could never get used to was the Apaches' burning, looting, and torturing. Once he had watched with fear and horror as they skinned alive a farmer who had defiled an Apache girl, tensed to his screams, unable to share their grinning pleasure. The warrior who had performed this trick was Kothluni.

'Jesus!' A startled hiss came from Rattler. 'That's him.'

A line of some thirty or forty Apaches had appeared like silent ghosts on the brow of a rocky rise, their flapping white shirts belted at the waist, their faces and lithe bare thighs blackened by exposure to the weather. Most wore buckskin moccasins laced to the knee. They carried carbines, or simple bows, and quivers packed with a hundred arrows. Most were on foot, the Apache's favourite mode of fighting and stepped through the rocks on either side of the trail. But along that came five of them on sturdy ponies led by Kothluni.

It had been seven years since Rattler had seen him last, but it was unlikely he could forget his hunched, powerful shoulders and arms, the crimson rag he wore around his head like a turban, the grim, ugly set of his features, the way he sat his horse scenting the air like a hawk seeking prey. And it returned to him, too, the way Kothluni had grinned his twisted teeth as he hung a captive soldier head down over a fire. Rattler shuddered, involuntarily, at the memory. Kothluni saw no reason to kill his prisoners quickly. They should be made to suffer first.

The horses had been herded far back down the trail and left with three troopers. The rest of the soldiers had tried to brush out the horse tracks and their own footprints in the dust before taking cover. But there was always the chance they had left some tell-tale sign. However, they were a seasoned platoon and knew how to keep their heads down, stay calm under duress. Their mudcaked uniforms and beards blended in with the tangle of the under-growth. Most hadn't taken a bath for three months or more and Rattler was thankful they were downwind of the desert breeze, otherwise, the Apaches would have smelled them by now. Would their sharp eyes notice anything amiss?

For Lieutenant Prendergast it was his first ever taste of action, his first sight of a hostile, and he looked scared. He was licking his dry lips and wiping the sweat from his palms. Sgt Rattler half-expected him to get up and run. The sweat on his own back turned chill as he watched the warriors step down from the rocks and, bunched behind their leader, cautiously approach through the ravine.

Tribollet played his part well. He lounged back on the box, his top hat tipped over his nose, and yawned as if awoken from a pleasant snooze. 'Howdy, boys,' he called. He had nerve, Rattler had to give him that.

He had broken into pigeon Apache, indicating the broken wheel that had been rolled to one side. He had a bottle of his own hooch in his hand, and offered it to Kothluni. 'Here, try this.'

The leader of the renegades, Kothluni, glanced about him at the rocky, scrub-lined ravine as if he suspected something. But the Apaches' love of whiskey, as strong as their love of gambling, (in some ways they were little different to the white man) made them reckless. They crowded around Kothluni and watched eagerly as he took a good drink.

Kothluni nodded seriously, took a heavy sack from across his horse's neck and tossed it to Tribollet. The latter gave a toothy leer as he peered inside, slung it across his shoulder, and jumped down. The warriors gave wild yelps of joy as they swarmed around the back of the wagon and began hoisting out the cases of whiskey.

Tribollet unhitched one of the mules, swung aboard, saluted Kothluni, and set off at a stiff-legged lope along the ravine. Whether it was the haste of his departure, or Kothluni had detected the gleam of sunshine on the lieutenant's polished gilt buttons, or on a carbine barrel, but he gave a piercing warning scream and charged his pony after Tribollet.

'Fire!' Sgt McMullan bellowed, not waiting for the lieutenant's command.

And, without further ado, the soldiers did so, a volley of carbine and revolver fire barking out from behind rocks and Spanish bayonet. Johnny Rattler, however, was watching Kothluni, who had sprinted his horse alongside Tribollet, back-swung a tomahawk, cracked him across the forehead, knocking him from the mule. The warrior chief leaped down onto the struggling Tribollet, and, his face transfixed with hatred at this white man's treachery, he carved the tomahawk into his skull.

Rattler had his carbine aimed at Kothluni. It was a long shot. He had him in his sights, but, for some reason, he did not squeeze the trigger. He watched with fascinated horror as his father was hacked to death, his scalp ripped from his head. When Kothluni waved the bloody hair in triumph it was then Rattler fired. At the same moment the Apache moved to grab his horse and the bullet scorched his arm. It was enough, however, to make him drop the scalp and to back away with his horse behind the shelter of some rocks.

'Hot damn!' Rattler cried, as he pressed another shell into the breech. 'I coulda had him then.'

All hell had broken out in the ravine. The Apache, besieged on both sides, were leaping back and forth like bobtail rabbits, seeking cover, firing their bows and rifles from the kneel, and bobbing away again.

'Why don't they stand still?' McMullan moaned as he missed once more. They were damned difficult targets.

Lead whined and ricocheted off the rocks, clouds of black gunpowder smoke rolled, and the air was pervaded with sulphur as the troopers cut the Apache down. The savages were getting the worst of it, many toppling in their tracks. But the troopers were also in danger from bullets fired wildly by their counterparts on the far side of the ravine.

An Irish corporal beside Rattler gave a

gasp of surprise as an arrow thudded into his chest. He fell back, writhing with pain and, before Rattler could stop him, had broken off the haft with his hands. He lay staring at it as if he knew it was a fool thing to do.

Kothluni was charging back along the ravine, hung low over his horse's head, screaming to his men to retreat. Bullets whistled and whanged about him, but as always, he led a charmed life. He disappeared over the rise and the warriors, those left on their feet, began dodging after him, firing as they ran.

Suddenly they were gone and silence reigned. There was only the whine of the desert wind, the smell of sulphur and blood. The troopers began to emerge from their hiding places, shouting to each other as they scrambled down the slope. Several slung carbines over their shoulders, pulled hunting knives and began darting back and forth among the wounded Apache, eager to finish them off.

Johnny Rattler went with them and paused to kneel over a youth he had once played with as a boy. 'Hi!' he said, and grinned at him. The youth stared at him, impassive in the face of death. A trooper pushed past, tried to slit the boy's throat. Rattler knocked up his arm. 'Leave him,' he said. 'He'll make a good scout.' He helped the youth hobble to one side and propped him up against a rock, tied his own red bandanna around his forehead to show he was enrolled.

But, Rattler had no aversion to take scalps from the dead Indians, and turned to take trophies.

'Stop this,' Prendergast screamed. 'Stop this disgraceful conduct, Sergeant!'

He slapped with the flat of his sabre at Rattler, who was carving away an Apache's long, black hair. Rattler looked up and scowled at Prendergast. 'You know how much these go for in Tombstone? Fifty dollar, maybe more.'

'That's no excuse. We're not savages, man.

Sergeant, we've got to get after them. Give the order.'

'Ach, what's the use?' McMullan was lighting his pipe. 'They'll all break up, disappear into the thorn, regroup some place else. Yon 'pache can run faster than any horse in this country.'

Rattler strolled away towards his father's body a hundred yards along the trail. He rolled him over with his boot, stared at him, thoughtfully. Blood trickled from his tomahawked head and his mouth was drawn back in a grim rictus of pain.

'Don't say you didn't ask for it,' he said, with a bitter grimace. He picked up the sack Kothluni had given Tribollet, weighed it in his hand. A quick peek inside told him it was probably the spoils of the raid on the Tombstone stage four weeks before: dollars in gold, silver and notes, necklaces encrusted with diamonds, bracelets, gold watches, wallets, rings. There had been some wealthy passengers on board. This was why the cavalry had come out looking for

Kothluni in the first place. He glanced back at the soldiers, strode up among the rocks, stuffed the sack into a hole.

When he strolled back McMullan suddenly became suspicious. 'What were you doin' up there? What happened to that sack Tribollet was given?'

'No sign of it. Kothluni musta snatched it back.'

'I said, "What happened to that sack?"' McMullan roared, bull-like, aware that he'd been slow off the starting line.

'Search me. Kothluni musta taken it back.'

'One of these days I'm gonna fix you.' McMullan pointed a finger at him. 'You're as crafty a bastard as that mongrel Tribollet was.'

Johnny Rattler smiled at him, mockingly, as Prendergast said, 'Come along, Sergeant, don't start gossiping. I want all these bodies buried.'

'We don't bury Apaches, sor. We leave 'em for the coyotes. We only lost two of our boys. We should take 'em back to camp for a military funeral.'

The lieutenant raised his arms with a hopeless shrug at the desolate scene of carnage. 'What about the corporal? He's in a bad way.'

'He won't last to morning,' Rattler said. 'There's no way you can get that arrow head out.'

'Maybe we can repair the wagon, sor. Transport Corporal McGinty and the dead men back in it.'

This they did, only the stricken McGinty complaining that he did not want to ride amid corpses.

'Aw, shut up,' McMullan said, hefting Tribollet in on top of him. 'You'll be one yourself soon enough.'

Two

Pearl Holm was lying on her bed half-naked in only a Stetson hat and pantalettes, playing a kind of Russian roulette. The window was wide open but the evening air hardly stirred. The sun had beat all day on the clapboard walls of her parents' dry goods store and the rooms of their living accommodation above had become as sultry and warm as an oven. Pearl wiped a trickle of sweat from between her pale breasts. They were firm and uptilted, young girl's breasts, wide aureolas about their pink nipples. She looked down at her unblemished body, her belly, her smooth, shapely legs. The sort of body men hungered for. She knew that by the way they looked at her in the street, especially when she wore the peekaboo blouse her mother scolded her about.

Pearl was bored. She had a deep longing for excitement, for 'life'. And there she was stuck in that oven-hot house with her boring parents. She lit one of the cigarettes she had stolen from the display shelf and let it hang from her full, cherubic lips. She picked up the .41 calibre Colt Cloverleaf revolver, slipped one leg off the bed and manoeuvred so she could see herself in the wardrobe mirror again. Instead of pointing the gun at her temple as in proper roulette, she aimed it at her image. She held her breath, squeezed the trigger, heard the click as the hammer went home on an empty cylinder. She scowled, let the smoke trickle from her lips and spun the Colt on one finger. She smiled, sensually, at her image. She knew there was a slug in there. There would be hell to play if she hit the wardrobe, smashed the glass. But she did not care. She aimed and clicked the cylinder around once more. She could always say she didn't know it was loaded.

There was a hammering on the door.

'What you doing in there, Pearl? I can smell smoke. You been stealing cigarettes again? What you got the door locked for?'

'What you doing in there, Pearl?' she mimicked, smiling. 'If she only knew.'

'What you doing in there, Pearl?' Her mother was rattling the handle. 'Open this door this minute.'

'What you think I'm doing?' she called. 'I'm reading my Bible. I don't want to be disturbed. I just reached a good bit 'bout Jezebel.'

'Just you wait 'til your father gets back. You're not too old for a thrashing. Now, open up.'

Why don't they leave me alone? she thought. Forever nagging. They won't let me go out. And they won't give me any peace when I'm in. 'I've worked hard all day, dammit,' she shouted. 'I'm entitled to lie down and relax.'

'Be a good girl,' her mother whined.

A good girl? She was a good girl. Fat chance she had of being otherwise. She did

36

her chores, served in the store, helped with the cooking, washing, goat-milking, and they watched her like a couple of hawks. She guessed that was what came from being the only child. They were scared of her running off, going to the bad. They didn't want her mixing with the town boys, or other riff-raff. They seemed to think they owned her, body and soul, that it was her duty to stay with them, take over the store, look after them in their old age. They didn't realize that their constant moralizing made her feel more rebellious than ever. It was not as if they were holier than anyone else. While quoting the Bible her hypocritical mother would be stingily short-weighing a customer's bacon. Her father that evening had taken the wagon out to the San Carlos reservation. Up to no good. Everybody knew that. Doing some deal with the agent, Tiffany, depriving the Indians of their rations.

Over supper they had been bickering at her again. Two against one. No, she couldn't go to the dance hall. Not on her own. Did she want to turn out like those young hussies along there? They all knew what *they* were like. She wasn't some tomboy any more, running about in blue jeans and shirt, helping the men down at the corral to break the broncs. She was growing up. She needed men to respect her. How else would she meet a decent man, not some ne'er-do-well? They were church-going folk. They had built up this business through hard work ... on and on they went. Did they never cease? She was nearly sixteen and they treated her like a child!

'I'm willing to take you to the dance if I chaperon you, Pearl.' Her mother was back again outside the door. 'But you're not going on your own.'

'Who do you think you are, some fat Mexican mama? Chaperone, indeed!' she shouted. 'Why do you treat me like a kid? Go away. I want to sleep.'

She listened, and jumped to her feet, pulling on the peekaboo blouse her mother didn't like, and black stockings, which she pinned above her knees with red garters. It was too hot for them, really, but she guessed she had to look ladylike at her age. She buttoned her ankle boots, cast off her Stetson, and put on a wide, be-ribboned hat. She climbed daringly out of the window into the branches of a cottonwood tree, eased along its bough and slid to the ground. She brushed herself down and smiled. Free!

The town of Globe served the copper mines and outlying farmsteads of the San Carlos valley. Its main street was a wide dusty curve of false-fronted stores and houses. Pearl hurried along the wooden sidewalk and her heart leapt when she saw the sign, 'Jake's Dance Hall'. In the gathering dusk tar flares had been lit outside. There were buggies and hitched horses. And she could hear the crashing sound of music, see the silhouettes of young people standing outside. It attracted Pearl like a moth to the flame. It was an oasis of light and laughter. It excited her as if she were about to enter a pool of temptation.

She paused to light a cigarette and strolled up to the doorway as if she were just passing by. 'Look who's here!' It was the voice of a scrawny school acquaintance, Mary Knowles. Her people were nester scum. She was sitting swinging her legs from a hitching rail, talking to two boys. 'Who let you out?'

'They didn't.' Pearl paused beside her and pretended not to notice the boys. 'I escaped.'

'Look at her smoking.' One of the spotty-faced boys looked shocked. It was not the thing any decent woman did in public. 'Looks like a damn hoo-er.'

'Don't be so provincial.' Pearl blew a streak of smoke out at the boy. 'You want one?'

They delved into the proffered packet, eagerly.

'What's the band like? Many in there?'

'Aw, mainly a few ole married frumps swingin' each other round. As if they can't do that at home.'

'Sounds OK to me.' Pearl tapped her foot, moved her hips, eager to get in there, but nervous. She didn't want to make it obvious she was out on her own. People might get the wrong idea. 'Coming in, Mary?'

'In a minute. When it gets warmed up. It's nice and cool out here.'

Most of the men going in and out looked like miners or ranch hands. Like the two hicks smoking her cigarettes they had brilliantined down their unruly hair, tied stubby ties around the collars of their worn workshirts tucked into their concertina pants. Cornsuckers!

It was at that moment that a rider on a glossy chestnut came galloping into town, pursued by two whooping Apaches. Everybody turned to look, for moments fearing the worst. Then they saw they were army scouts and they spat or pretended in-difference. Soldiers were not regarded in the most favourable light.

The leading rider reined in in a swirl of

dust close to the girls and gave them a flashing smile from beneath his black cavalry hat. Pearl's body tensed with excitement and her blue eyes seemed to flash sparks off his dark ones in the torch blaze. She had never before seen such a handsome youth; there was a delicacy to the lines of his face, his wide suntanned brow, his glossy black hair, his neat nostrils and firm chin. He wore a white cotton shirt open to the night, tight twill cavalry pants tucked into cork-soled fringed leggings. He controlled the snorting horse with his knees as it pranced to and fro.

'Hi,' he called, 'is this where the baile is? I'm fandango crazy.'

'Me, too.' Pearl smiled lazily, leaned against the hitching rail with her cigarette. She squealed as he pushed the horse up close. 'Careful! It ain't horses I want squashing me.'

Mary tittered and nudged her. 'Pearl, you're surely terrible.'

'Cain't you see the sign?' one of the youths

glowered. 'No dogs, no Injins. That's what it says.'

'Don't you worry about my boys. They know how to behave. They brought their own booze and gonna dance in the street.'

The two scouts, in their cavalry jackets and red headbands, grinned at him as they sat on a water trough and produced a bottle.

'With that long hair,' one of the boys uttered, 'you look like a durn Injin yourself.'

'Me? I got aristocratic French blood in me mixed with southern Yankee, but I must admit my granny was a Yaqui. Just remember, half-wit, if it weren't for men like me and those boys you people wouldn't be sleeping easy in your beds.'

'Where you get this beaut of a horse?' Pearl was fondling the chestnut's ears as he chomped on the bit. 'This ain't your average cavalry plug.'

'He sure ain't. This here's Amigo. So happened I bought him from a deal I did in Tombstone selling 'pache scalps. Me an' the boys took 'em personally, ourselves, a few days ago. Maybe you read about it in the paper?'

'Kothluni? Was that your outfit?'

'Sure was.' Rattler smiled to himself – why shouldn't he boast a bit? 'How about you, pretty gal? Fancy a ride on this thang? He goes like a rocket outa hell.'

'I ain't dressed.' Pearl drew back as he held out his arm. Then she pulled up her skirt and he swung her up behind him, and she gripped Rattler around the waist. She could see the boys trying to get a peek up her dress at her pantalettes, and to look disapproving at the same time. 'OK, let's go.'

She screamed as he shot away. The chestnut certainly did go. She could feel his power drumming through her as they went tearing up the dusty street. She gripped her hat as the wind tore at her hair and hung on for dear life. An excitement flowed through her as she hugged herself into the youth's back, an excitement more to do with the feel of the man than the horse. They went on out of town, out under the stars, the hooves thudding their tattoo. Pearl felt delirious. She wanted to go on for ever. She was quite disappointed when Johnny Rattler pulled hard in, laughing, out of breath and set the horse back at a lope.

'You OK?' he called.

'I surely am,' she said, nestling her nose into his ear.

'You're only a kid. What you doing out on your own like this? Howja know you can trust me?'

'I don't,' she whispered, but he didn't take the hint.

He took her back to Mary and the boys and she jumped down, smiling. Rattler unsaddled Amigo and busied himself at the water trough sponging him down. 'I look after my horses,' he said.

He turned to Pearl and took her by the hand. 'How about a jig with me?' He flipped a dollar to the boy on the door and led her into Jake's Dance Hall. It was jam-packed. 'Come on.' He swept her into the swirl of whirling bodies. It wasn't exactly a Viennese waltz. It was fast and furious, a fantastic cacophony kicked up by the squeeze-box, fiddle, blaring trumpet and thumping Indian drum. To Pearl it seemed like heaven as she clung to her beau, and, some fancy stepper, he guided her energetically through the maze of spinning taffeta dresses and stomping boots.

Five dances later she begged for a rest and he pushed their way through the beaming, sweat-streaming faces, out into the yard. He pulled her into the shadows and encircled her soft, warm body with his arms, stooping to kiss her. Pearl clung to his strong shoulders, surrendering her body, glued tight to him. She had never been kissed before like this. She felt giddy with joy. This was divine, delicious, absolutely...

'Pearl! Pearl! Where are you?' Mary Knowles stuck her nose out of the door and screeched, 'Your father's coming down the street. He's carryin' a shotgun.'

'Oh, my God!' Pearl felt quite dizzy as she

pulled away from Rattler. 'I gotta go. I'm sorry.'

She groped her way through the reeling and rocking dancers, reached the door. It was true. Her father was forty yards away and he looked like he meant business. She jammed her hat on her head and walked with quick, nimble steps towards him. He beckoned her past him with the shotgun, made a motion to cuff her. She hurried on home. How humiliating! Rounded up like some stray animal. She knew those boys were laughing.

Rattler stood and watched them go, shrugged and took a swig from his Apache friends' whiskey bottle. There were plenty more girls, but there was something about her...

Three

The two Apache boys were drunk, rolling in the dust, fighting each other, a crowd of rowdy onlookers gathered around, aiming kicks to encourage them. Johnny Rattler waded in, pulled them apart. Luckily they hadn't yet got round to knives. 'Give us a hand sober 'em up,' he yelled. He was worried the crowd outside Jake's Dance Hall might get nasty and lynch his scouts. Willing hands dragged the boys apart, dunking them again and again in the horse trough. As Jack Seven Clouds came up spluttering, Rattler cried, 'Hang on, don't drown the poor bastard. You had enough, Jack?' The Apache nodded mutely, his hair in his eyes.

It was odd how quickly an Indian got drunk. Something to do with their bodies

48

not being able to absorb the sugar content. They staggered mightily, but once on their broncs were fine. No Apache ever fell off a horse unless he was shot off.

'Come on, boys,' he shouted. 'We got work to do.' And he led them galloping out of town.

They rode at a hard lope through the moonlit hills towards the Dragoons, through the mesquite, sagebrush and yucca bathed in a silver glow, rode towards the ragged dark outlines of the border mountains. At the first flush of dawn they rested their tired horses, lit a low fire, boiled up crushed coffee beans in their tin cups, and roasted a jack-rabbit over the embers. One of the boys had brained it with a stick. They found some shade and rolled up in their saddle blankets to sleep through the heat of the day. As dusk descended they set off again into hostile country. At midnight they paused to water their broncs, digging with a stick into a dry wash until a small pool of water appeared. And it was lucky for them they did. They heard the drumming of hooves and, crouching down, saw the dark silhouettes of a pack of Apache prowling along the trail.

'Whee!' Rattler gave a low whistle. 'We coulda run slap into 'em. Wouldn'ta given much for our chances if we had. What a way to spend a furlough. Remember, boys, there's whiskey in this for you.'

This was crazy. What a man would do for gold! But they rode on for another two nights across the hard land until they struck the trail. The sun was beginning to rise high as they approached the ravine where the fight with Kothluni had been. At first Johnny Rattler thought he heard dogs barking, but it was black-headed vultures tearing at the last remains of the twenty warriors who had died, only their heads were not black but reddened by blood. Kothluni hadn't been back to claim them. That was one way the Apache differed from the northern tribes like the Sioux. They didn't waste time wailing over the departed.

They'd hold a special ceremony for their spirits later on in the year. This place would be avoided now as a place of ghosts. The kit-foxes and coyotes had had a feast, but there were still a few pickings left for the birds.

The three friends watched them for a few moments as they hopped and squabbled about their gory breakfast. Rattler gave an involuntary shudder and went to search for the hole. 'Hot damn!' he hissed. 'Somebody has been here before me.'

No! He searched some more and found the sack hidden further up in the rocks. Eagerly, he counted out the gold and silver coins – $422 in all. The Apache boys were more interested in the jewellery and trinkets. Rattler bagged a gold hunter watch. The half-enclosed face gave it more protection in a fall. It was engraved inside to somebody called Hiram C. Nates, doubtless now deceased. He gave the boys $100 each and they seemed well-pleased. Fair enough.

'Let's git back to civilization while we still got our scalps,' he grinned. 'If we go on like this we're gonna git rich. I'll be able to buy myself a saloon.'

They made good time back across the line, narrowly avoiding a large patrol of *rurales*, who would have given them short shrift and sold their scalps down in Chihuahua.

They eased up once they were back on the American side and headed for Tombstone. They still had three days to spend before they were due back at Fort Bowie.

A purple dusk illumined the clapboard houses like stage settings against the lonesome desert as they rode their broncs down the wide main street of Tombstone. The tinkling of piano, the gentle strains of guitar, and the scraping of bull fiddle drifted from numerous beer parlours and saloons, mingling with raucous laughter and halloos as the population began to make ready for the night's festivities. Tombstone was built on silver, but in the wake of the honest miners and traders had come a host of hard-eyed jackals looking for easier pickings. The great South-west had no shortage of drifters, desperadoes, con-men, gamblers, thieves, idlers, pickpockets, muggers and prostitutes seeking the main chance. And to cater for the lusts and thirsts of a floating population of 30,000 souls, if souls they had, there were no less than 100 saloons, beer parlours and gambling bells.

They put Rattler's chestnut and the Apaches' sturdy piebald ponies into the OK Corral, scene of a shootout a couple of years before, and ambled over to the smithy's. It was a good place to get the lowdown on a town.

'Who's runnin' Tombstone these days? You got a lawman here?'

The big blacksmith dunked a red-hot shoe to sizzle in a bucket and gave them the once over. 'Sure. New law court's jest bin built. All sorts of jackals in top hats and frock coats battening down. The sheriff spends most his time chasin' taxes, settling mine claims, 'stead of taking on the pimps and card sharps, the rustlers and hoss thieves. Why, you plannin' on holdin' up the bank?'

'Not jest yet,' Rattler grinned. 'Which sheriff's that?'

'Ever heard of Perry Owens, one-time deputy of Apache County? You can't miss him, he's got hair down past his shoulders and he's armed to the teeth.'

'Man jest likes to know whose toes not to step on,' Rattler said. 'What happened to Mr Earp?'

'Wyatt?' The smithy put the shaggy hoof of the carthorse into his leather lap. 'That fast-talkin' dandy got outa here. Too many old scores bein' settled. Too many of the Clanton clan lookin' for revenge. One Earp brother, Morgan, dead, another Virgil, crippled. Doc Holliday coughing his last in a Colorado clinic. Without them alongside him Wyatt was nobody. Why, boys, you fancy yourselves as fast guns?'

'Not 'zactly. Jest fancy a good time. They serve my 'pache boys in this town?'

'Sure,' the blacksmith boomed out. 'They

serve anybody got a silver dollar. Even Chinks in their skull caps and pigtails. If they serve them they'll serve anybody.'

'You give our horses a bucket of grain? We come a long way.'

The smithy couldn't reply because he'd got a mouthful of nails in his teeth. He merely winked when Johnny Rattler stuffed a greenback in his grimy wool vest.

Away from the ramshackle wooden town was the old Mexican village of narrow streets and adobe houses, yellow flowers sprouting from the flat roofs. From inner courtyards came the sound of laughter and voices, the whine of a mandolin, spicy food smells drifting to their nostrils. Not so long before this whole territory had been part of the Spanish Empire, and old customs died hard.

They pushed through bead curtains down steps into a shady half-cellar called Rosita's Cantina. The tables and chairs were of rough wood and the clientele mostly dark Mexican, some in the white cotton pyjamas and sombreros of peons, other harder-looking men dressed *vaquero*-style, striped serapes over their shoulders, and strung with shooting irons. These eyed them, suspiciously. A bitter hatred had existed between Mex and Apache for 300 years. But, seeing Rattler's army stripes, they let it go, returned to their own affairs. The food was good, hot and fiery. Stewed beef fifty cents; coffee five cents.

Rattler was pouring them tequila when a slim Spanish girl slid onto his knee, wound a strong wiry arm around his neck. 'Aaiiee! *Hombre!* You got dreenk for me?'

'She musta smelled my dollars,' Rattler said, smiling as he glanced around. The gringos were not the only ones into horse stealing, prostitution, smuggling and other nefarious activities. This was a real greaser low-life hide-out. He poured her a glass as her long black curls brushed his cheek. 'Make yourself comfortable, *señorita*.' He pulled her more securely into him. Her bare bronzed legs snaking from the flounces of her crimson dress were like whipcord, and the same went, he reckoned, for her hard little buttocks.

'*Querido mio,*' she crooned in his ear, snatching up a ten dollar greenback he'd laid down for the food and drink. 'You geev me thees, huh?'

She had stuffed the note into the soft shadowy valley of her breasts, into the depths of her loose blouse, before he could regain it.

'Me an' the boys was lookin' more for a bed to sleep.'

'Sure, you sleep later. Beds three dollar. Me five dollar.'

'Kinda pricey, aincha?'

'*Si*, but I geev you good.' And she grabbed him hard by the back of his neck and pressed her mouth onto his, her teeth grinding, before she slipped her tongue down his throat to kinda prove her point.

'Hold on, honey. Let me finish my coffee. We ain't been introduced. What's your handle?'

'Conchita.' Her sultry brown eyes smiled into his and she licked his nose. 'You like me?'

'She's got a tongue like a lizard, this gal. I think we'll be OK here, boys. Conchita, you look after my Apache chums, too?'

She wrinkled her nose up in distaste as she surveyed them, and shrugged. '*Si*. Five dollar, too.'

The girl hauled Rattler to his feet and dragged him towards a back room. It was a simple whitewashed room with a bed, bucket, bowl and jug, an icon of the Virgin flickering in an alcove. Conchita briefly crossed herself and fell back onto the coverlet, laughing as she waved her toe in the air. 'Ride me, *hombre*,' she cried. 'Ride me.'

Four

Two days after tequila, mescal, sweet warm beer, two nights of trying to kick the tiger at the faro table, or Conchita's lascivious, slick-tongued attentions, had begun to take its toll. Johnny Rattler was jaded, his nerves on edge. He and the boys stepped into the OK Saloon about noon and ordered breakfast. At night the place would be swarming with miners who had struck paydirt and were busy getting rid of it fast. They were an international brigade, Poles, Italians, Cornishmen, Pennsylvanians, in their dusty Levi denims, arrived with their mokes and picks to hack at the rock. At this time of day they would be out at the mines. There was only a sprinkling of city slickers in bowler hats and four-button suits, sporting walrus moustaches, the fashion of the day, rubbing shoulders with farmers in battered Stetsons and workworn clothes, baggy britches tucked into boots. In the evening the troupe of girls would be shrieking and cartwheeling on stage, but now a flurry of them lounged about at the empty tables immodestly showing their befrilled drawers, tugging a comb through tangled locks, looking wan and worn after their hard night.

Rattler ordered up flapjacks and honey, and hot black coffee. Jack Seven Clouds got stuck into the vittles. Blue Owl sat depilating himself, plucking out the hairs of his brows, and anything that spoilt the smoothness of his chin. Apache women couldn't abide hairy men, but both had long black hair hanging down over the faded shoulders of their cavalry coats for Apaches believed it to be the source of their power; to crop it would bring disaster.

'What them stinkin' Injins doin' in here?'

The voice echoed across the saloon. Johnny Rattler flinched slightly but carried on chewing. He saw a rum-soaked former Rebel, a so-called 'Major' Oates leaning against the bar. He sported a dowdy grey Confederate frock coat, and black campaign hat. He had one boot on the brass rail and was peering over his shoulder at them, little pig eyes in a flushed face, a moth-eaten beard.

'These stinkin' Injins is with me: "A" Company of the Third Cavalry,' Rattler growled. 'An' if there's anybody stinkin' up the joint it's you.'

'Anybody goes round with Injins must be a stinkin' snake himself. I'd rather have a rattler in my coat pocket than an Apache.'

Seven Clouds took a sip of his coffee. 'This man try to spoil my breakfast.'

'Take it easy, boys,' Rattler smiled.

Blue Owl was still plucking his eyebrows, peering into a little mirror, his face a dark mask. They called them redskins, but an Apache's skin was almost black.

'White wimmin, children, massacred on the stage at Willow Springs three weeks ago and he comes in here bold as brass with these mothers,' Oates was muttering at the bar.

Rattler finished his meal, pushed the plate away, put his feet up on a chair and picked at his teeth with a broken match. He flipped a ten dollar bill down for the food, and counted his wad. 'Twenty-five left, boys. Where the hell did it all go?'

He knew where it had gone. Across the bar, at the faro table, on the Wheel of Fortune. And Conchita had got her sticky little fingers on a good hitch of it. 'Don't know what my daddy would say wasting my inheritance like this. How about you, Jack?'

Jack Seven Clouds felt in his pocket and produced five silver dollars and a few cents. Blue Owl had started to eat and merely shook his head, negatively.

'We can't have blown four hundred, surely? Can we? Jeez, it's time we headed back to camp. We've had our fun.'

Major Oates, and two surly cronies, had

come to stand over them. 'What's the matter, sweetheart? Can't you pay your bill?'

'Yeah, we can pay our bill. We jest ain't been on a winnin' streak, thassall.'

'How much you got?' Oates leaned across and counted the dollars with a crooked finger. 'Twenty-five? Well, I'll do you stinkin' bastards a favour and take it offen you. Then you git your smelly carcasses outa here.' He sat down on a chair at the table, produced a greasy pack of cards and flipped them out in front of him. 'What's it to be?'

'OK.' Rattler shrugged. 'Let's make it aces high.'

They played, and nobody could blame the liquor this time, but inevitably, it seemed, he watched his remaining dollars go. The two men gave sneering guffaws, and "Major" Oates grinned, 'Aincha got nuthin' else to bet?'

Oates was one of those soldier bores, forever telling how he had joined General Sibley's southern army in New Mexico, and reliving his heroic role in the battle of Gloriette Pass, near Santa Fe, twenty years before, as if he were the only one who had fought in that conflagration that split the nation, the most terrible war known to humanity. Since then he had lived by his sneaking wits. Rattler knew he was cheating. Where, did his aces keep coming from?

'You oughta be publicly flogged for sedition, you lousy, loudmouthed Reb,' was all he could think of to say. He had read that in a news-sheet someplace.

'Major' Oates's cunning face registered surprise for a moment, before he sneered, 'Hark to him, he don't like losing. These Injins and 'breeds ain't got much juice in their coconuts. Come on, you pretty boys must have somethin' else to bet?'

'I ain't a 'breed,' Rattler replied, huffily. He disliked that word. He wasn't ashamed of his Yaqui grandmother, probably she was the only decent woman among his progenitors, but nobody liked being called that. 'My mama was an all-American woman, and better'n any you Tennessee trash.'

'Yeah, I remember her when she used to hang around Tucson after Tribollet. Even he had no use for her. She was no damn good as a mother or as a hoo-er. I should know, I riveted her often enough.'

A small crowd had drifted over from the bar to watch, and guffawed at this. Folks loved a slander match. Anger burned in Rattler at this slight to his mother, but he controlled himself 'Maybe she made a bad choice of profession,' he muttered.

'Don't you worry, honey,' one of the girls chimed in. 'She musta been a martyr. I been with the major and it was the most disappointing two minutes of my career.'

Everybody laughed some more as Oates scowled, speechless. Meanwhile Blue Owl was digging in the pockets of his cavalry jacket for something to bet. He produced with a grin a diamond necklace, bracelet and matching earbobs, and tossed them onto the table. Not to be outdone Seven Clouds took a treble string of pearls from the wampum around his own throat.

There was a sudden silence as they all studied the valuable jewellery.

'Oh, shee-it!' Rattler growled.

'Whew!' Major Oates picked up the items and whistled with awe. 'These are *some* jewels. Where'd you get 'em, you thievin' snakes?'

'Hang on a minute!' One of the dudes in a derby leaned over and took the items, holding them aloft to sparkle in the light. 'These look mighty like the stuff stolen from those women massacred on the coach. I work at the law courts. Somebody had better go get the sheriff.'

'Yeah.' Oates gave a malicious, grinning snarl. 'I shouldn't be surprised if these three didn't do that robbery and blame it on Kothluni.'

'Don't be stupid,' Johnny Rattler said. 'Kothluni gave it to my father, Jacques Tribollet, before he killed him. This is my inheritance. How was I to know where it come from? Anyway, it's the spoils of war.'

'A good legal point, kid,' another dude put in. 'You'll be needing a lawyer. Here's my card.'

'The sheriff's outa town,' a surly-looking, unshaven oaf alongside the Major shouted. 'I vote we try these three and hang 'em now.'

'No,' Oates said. 'I ain't countenancing no lynch law. We'll hold these boys until he gets back. Then we'll hang 'em.' Oates produced a single-shot .31 calibre derringer from his flounced sleeve and as he did so two aces fell out. 'You young skunks better come quiet now.'

'Nobody hangs me, you cheating bastard!' Rattler went for his shoulder-hung single action .44-.40 Lightning, and leapt to one side from his chair. As he cocked the Colt the derringer's slug burned his cheek. Instinctively, he replied, lead for lead. Oates staggered back and collapsed against the wooden wall, a large red hole in his forehead leaking blood.

The explosions reverberated about the big

barnlike saloon and, as the acrid black smoke drifted, Rattler hissed, 'Let him brag about that.'

The ugly pug, who had been in favour of a necktie party, pulled out a Remington from his belt. Before he could fire Blue Owl's tomahawk sliced open the top of his skull. He screamed and toppled back, his brain matter, the colour of stale bread, oozing onto the floor.

The bald, red-nosed barkeep produced a ten-gauge, its double barrels aimed at them. Jack Seven Clouds always kept his Springfield carbine laid across his knees. He fired from the hip and the 'keep went flying back, bringing a mirror, bottles and glasses crashing down on top of him in clattering commotion.

Pandemonium erupted as folks scrambled to get clear and men alerted by the shooting pushed in through the batwing doors. 'Come on,' Rattler shouted. He charged at the window, his arm raised over his eyes. He smashed through and rolled onto the sidewalk, quickly followed by the Apache boys who tumbled on top of him. They dived through the hitched horses and raced at a crouch across the dusty street as bullets whistled about their ears.

'What's goin' on?' the smithy asked as they ran into the livery.

'You'll find out soon enough,' Rattler said.

He slung his saddle over Amigo in the stall, cinched it tight, grabbed his bridle. He didn't have time to fix it on. He leaped into the saddle and guided the fiery chestnut with his knees and by its mane. The Apache boys were getting their mustangs from the OK Corral as some men came running. Rattler fired three shots over their heads to make them think twice. Amigo was raring to go and he gave him his head, hanging low as they went streaking out of town, the Apaches charging after him.

'Haaayii!' Rattler screamed.

He hadn't wanted trouble, and he was shocked by the suddenness of the shootings, but, nonetheless, a fine excitement thrilled through him as they raced out into the desert.

They lay on a ridge among some creosote bushes, and looked back. There was no sign of pursuit. An eagle spiralled lazily on warm thermals and the bushes filled the air with a spicy smell. A man should be just enjoying this wonderful peaceful scene, instead of lying there wondering what the hell to do. They had killed three men. And it was as if that fact had altered Johnny Rattler's life radically.

'Cap'n Hentig will know what to do,' he muttered. 'There's saloon fights every day. It ain't no big deal.'

He fixed the chestnut's bridle and they went on at a butt-breaking trot towards Fort Bowie. Where else was there to go? They were soldiers. It was their home; the only home Johnny Rattler had known since the age of twelve.

As they rode through a forest of twenty-foot-high saguaro cactus, their fluted, strangely convoluted arms crowned with blossoms, and avoided the smaller, ground-hugging, vicious cholla and cat-claw cactus, Rattler remembered his days roving with Kothluni's band ... he had been a boy of twelve when he went on his last raid. It had been a disaster. They had run into a company of cavalry. In the mêlée Rattler was knocked from his saddle and kicked in the head by a horse. He woke to find himself in the barracks hospital at Tucson.

Far from being grateful for his rescue, Johnny had been sullen and angry. He would as lief have stayed with the Apaches. He had come to regard them as his family. Where could he go now?

That question was answered for him by the rough but kindly soldiers. Without saying so, they adopted him at the garrison as their sort of mascot. They joshed him about his Apache ways, his name and speech. They bet on his ability to outshoot them with a bow and arrows. He could get flint-tips into a bottle neck from forty feet.

And they laughed at his preference for bareback riding, sending him out to round up their mounts.

The garrison commander, Captain George Hentig, had taken a fatherly interest, too, in the young 'captive'. In those days Hentig had been stepping out with a tempestuous Southern belle – Maureen O'Grady, a wealthy widow, who had a bit of a murky past. But the unlikely pair had seemed happy together, and the general opinion was that they would get hitched. Maureen, in her rustling silks, perfume and fashionable hats, was the epitome to Johnny Rattler of a 'lady', and she soon tamed the young 'Apache', wooing him back to being an American. She had taught him to read, and showed him how to fire her big old Stonewall Jackson six-shooter. Her father had been a gunsmith and had personally fashioned it for the Southern general, but he had died, shot accidentally by one of his own men, before he could collect it. They had some fine times together, going out on picnics and larking about, and it was the nearest thing Johnny had ever had to a real family. Unfortunately, something went wrong with the captain and Maureen's romance. She had put her money into running a swish gaming house and bordello, on the edge of Tucson, and maybe the captain couldn't stomach that. 'I'm an officer and gentleman, fer Christ's sake!' Rattler had once heard him exclaim. 'How can I marry the *madame* of a bordello?'

The two had parted, and Captain Hentig had been moved, at his own request, to command of the garrison at Fort Bowie, up out in the hills. He took the fourteen-year-old Rattler along with him and enrolled him as one of his scouts. Once, one evening, as he went to receive orders from him, he found Captain Hentig in his cabin with his boots stuck out in front of a spitting pine log fire, a glass of Irish whiskey in his hand, and the captain had muttered, 'A good bottle of whiskey's a better companion than any dang woman.'

But, he seemed a saddened, lonely man.

However, now known to most folks as Rattler, and, although scorned in the frontier racist way for being a 'quarter-breed', and for having consorted with savages, there was no doubting his youthful skill with revolver and rifle, knife and horse, and his ability to follow spoor and 'know' the enemy's moves. He proved so useful Captain Hentig had little hesitation in making him sergeant of scouts on his eighteenth birthday. He was put in charge of men much older than himself. Perhaps that was why Sergeant McMullan resented him so much?

It was a long ride, but they were used to long journeys in this land of distances, a hot and dreary ride going up the valley between the Santa Catalina mountains to the north and the Santa Ritas which stood out like purple cut-outs against the southern expanse of sky. Before them loomed the rough gradients of the Chiracahua Mountains, homeland of the Indians to whom he had once belonged and now was fighting against. They climbed higher and higher and soon could see the San Ignacio range running into the distance that was Mexico.

It gave Rattler plenty of time to think about his predicament, and that of his two fellow scouts. At one time, as they reined in, he was half-inclined to suggest that they made a dash for the border, sought refuge in that southern land. But no, the life of an outlaw was no life, every man's hand turned against you. One day Johnny Rattler hoped, or had hoped until now, that he would be able to save some cash, buy a small ranch, retire from the army, marry a decent gal, and raise a real family of his own. No, it was no good running. Cap'n Hentig would sort it out. One thing about it, old Sgt Mc-Mullan would have a laugh at their expense.

Fort Bowie was at an altitude of 4,800 feet, set amid a plain of grama grass, and consisted of some thirty rock and adobe buildings around the four sides of a quandrangle of fifteen acres.

'Talk of the devil,' Rattler said. 'Here he is.'

As they approached the fort Sgt Mc-Mullan appeared at the head of a company of troopers who came filing out of the gate in the stockade, jogging towards them.

'So, there y'are, ye three murtherin' coyotes,' McMullan shouted. 'Ye've made our job a lot easier. We were just setting out to look fer ye.'

McMullan ordered the troopers to a halt, and indicated them to surround the three scouts. 'I t'ought ye'd be headed for the border by now, boys. Hand over them weapons. Ye're under arrest.'

'Have you heard the news?' One of the troopers rode alongside. 'Geronimo's surrendered.'

'No!' Rattler was stunned. If he had it was the end of a lifetime of war, surely. 'You kiddin'?'

'No. Him and his warriors gave 'emselves up two days ago just south of the line. They're bringing him back.'

76

Rattler remembered the squat Chiracahua chief of enormous strength, his razor slit of mouth, and eyes like hard obsidian, nephew of Cochise, who had made the frontier a bloodbath for ten years past. He was getting old, fifty or sixty summers. Maybe he had just had enough.

'Kothluni won't give up so easy. He's younger.'

'He won't last long. We got orders to round up every Apache of warrior age. Cut away his support. General Miles is drafting in more men.'

General Nelson Miles, a fire and brimstone soldier, had taken over from the benign General George Crook, whose softgloved treatment of captured warriors had led to an outcry in the eastern Press and his resignation. Crook had tried to turn the Apaches into peaceful farmers, but the ring of traders who ran the Territory hadn't cottoned on to giving savages good land, to 'unfair competition', and had sabotaged his plans by every dirty trick in the book. Crook had retired, a disappointed man.

The blockhouse of Fort Bowie reared over them as they filed through the stockade gates, and the column came to a halt in the dusty barracks square.

'Throw 'em in the guardhouse,' Mc-Mullan roared.

After the days of hard-fighting, drinking and riding Rattler slept as if sandbagged even on the cell floor of pounded earth, bullock's blood and cactus juice that set like concrete. He awoke as the guard brought them coffee in tin canteens, and breakfast of weevil-crawling biscuits. They killed the weevils by dunking the hard tack in the scalding brew.

'You're up before Cap'n Hentig in an hour,' the guard said.

Hentig was a good officer, respected by his men, and was sitting behind his desk in shirt sleeves on account of the heat, his suspenders hanging down over his riding britches. Beside him was the shavetail lieutenant, Prendergast, his uniform immaculately brushed and polished and buttoned to the throat, his blond hair neatly clipped.

The captain shuffled some papers as Rattler, Jack Seven Clouds and Blue Owl were lined up before him. After a while of silence, he looked up and eyed them, severely. 'Well, boys, been getting yourselves into trouble, I hear. There's no way I can get you outa this. You can't go around shooting civilians' – he chuckled in a lower tone – 'much as I might personally like to, myself.'

He slapped Hiram C. Nates's gold hunter on his desk. 'You had this on you, Rattler. A clear indication that you've been up to no good.'

Rattler tried to explain about Tribollet's loot and what had occurred, but the captain hushed him. 'That was against army regulations, but is only the minor charge.'

Captain Hentig was a big, moustached man, his face and chest weatherbeaten by years on the frontier. 'We got a message on the talkin' wire' – that was for the Apaches' benefit, their word for telegraph – 'and it said you resisted arrest and each killed a man. I'm gonna read the charges out and hear what you got to say.'

'It was self-defence, Cap,' Rattler said.

'I doubt it,' Prendergast snapped. 'In my opinion this man is an undisciplined hothead. That stolen property should have been handed in to be returned to the relatives of the deceased.'

'What about the whiskey?' Rattler asked. 'Was that all handed in? I bet you had your share, didn't you, Cap?'

'That's nothing to do with it,' Hentig growled. He cleared his throat and glanced at his office cupboard inside which a dozen bottles were stashed. It was good stuff, even if it had given him one hell of a thumping head.

'I got more things to worry about than you small fry,' he muttered. 'I guess you've heard they've brought in that drunken, thieving murderer, Geronimo? We're putting him and his men in the railroad cars and shipping them to the dungeons of Pensacola, Florida.'

'Yeah?' Rattler didn't like the look on the captain's face. 'What's that got to do with us?'

'See here, Rattler,' Hentig sighed, pushed his chair back and stretched out his long legs. 'I've known you a long time. You've been a good sergeant, but you've over-stepped the mark this time. This Sheriff Owens is asking us to hand you over to the civil authorities. You know what will happen if I send you back? They'll stretch your necks for sure. That's the mood they're in.'

'So, you'll look after us, won't you, Cap?'

'I wish I could, but I can't. You damn frontier mongrels gotta learn. You can't go round shootin' up saloons any more. You three soldiers killed three civilians. That's that. You all been sure scouts, but the only way I can save your necks is ship you off with the other boys. At least in Florida you'll be able to talk about old times.'

'Geronimo will kill them as traitors. And

me, too. You know that.'

'That's the chance you took when you enrolled with the army.' Hentig rose and pulled on his uniform jacket. 'Guess I'd better make this official. Ain't no use arguing.'

He slumped back in his chair and poured some coffee as Lt Prendergast, in his haughty voice, read out the charges: 'Sgt John Rattler, or Tribollet, you are accused that...'

'Five years imprisonment,' Hentig intoned. 'At least you ain't being sent to that hell of Fort Yuma. Cheer up, boys. You'll still be young when you come out.'

'Take them away, Sgt McMullan,' Prendergast snapped. 'And *do* do up your buttons.'

The flush-faced Irishman saluted. 'Sor!' And began barking orders. 'The next part I'm gonna enjoy,' he grinned, as he shoved them out into the barracks square where a bevy of men had been hastily assembled.

A drum roll sounded, the men were called

to attention, with reversed arms as a sign of disgrace. Prendergast pronounced some high-falutin' words and stepped forward to rip off Rattler's stripes and cross-swords insignia hat. He stamped them into the dust. He did the same with Seven Clouds' and Blue Owl's hats, and ripped the buttons and badges from their coats. They were marched away to a barred cart to sit like caged animals, bare-headed in the sun, to await their fate.

Rattler saw Hentig watching from beneath the shaded wattle canopy outside his office. The captain turned on his heel and went back inside. 'Guess he reckons he's doing us a favour,' Rattler muttered.

Five

They had been squatting in their prison cage in the baking heat for about half an hour when Rattler spied a rider heading through the gates of the fort. He had long hair flowing to his shoulders beneath his stiff-brimmed hat, luxuriant moustachios, and was arrayed in fringed buckskins, a double-belt of bullets around his slim waist, and two long-barrelled Frontier .45s in tooled leather holsters.

'Howdy boys,' he called as he reined in before them, giving a sneering grin. 'So they've caught ya? Waal, saves me a job. All I gotta do now is take you back to Tombstone to have your necks stretched.'

'Too late, Sheriff. We already been sentenced under army law. We got five years apiece.'

'Yeah?' Sheriff Perry Owens's face darkened with anger beneath his tan. 'We'll see about that. You killed three civilians. I got prior claim on you.' He swung from his steamed-up bronc, left it to find its own way to a water trough, and strode over to the captain's office. He was a man of short stature, only about five-four, but with his chest, in the neat yoked shirt, stuck out belligerently, he had a determined air. He slammed the door as he pushed past the sentry and went inside.

'What's all this, George?' he cried. 'I told you to hold these men for me, not to court-martial 'em.'

'It's a *fait acompli*, as them Frenchies say, Perry.' Hentig glanced up from his desk. 'There ain't nuthin' you can do about it.'

'Oh, yes, there is. I'm taking them back to Tombstone. I got the legal right. And you ain't stopping me.'

'Come on, Sheriff, loosen up. You've had a long ride.' Hentig took a bottle of White Lightning from his drawer. 'Relax. This is a drop of good stuff. I got some more in the cupboard. Mebbe you'd like a coupla bottles?'

'Don't softsoap me, George. I got first option on them murderers. I'm gonna hang 'em. They can't come into my town shooting down innocent civilians.'

'Innocent civilians. Pah!' Hentig smacked his lips as he savoured a glass, and poured one for the lawman. 'You call that cheatin' jackanapes Oates an innocent civilian? He shoulda been drilled before now for his card-dealing ways. He pulled a piece on Rattler and lost the argument. It was a straightforward saloon brawl. And that piece of offal side-kick of his, waal, he'd been asking for it for a long time.'

'That's all very well.' Owens reached out, took the whiskey, and shot it back down his throat. He gasped and breathed out, 'Yeah, that ain't so bad.'

'Tribollet came up trumps for once before he left us. It ain't his usual poison.' Hentig proffered the bottle. 'Have another?'

Owens watched it poured and took the next one more gently. 'Yes, not so bad at all. But look here, Cap, what about our bar-keep? He was a popular man. Tombstone people want a reckoning for that.'

'He pulled a shotgun on 'em. He shouldn't have been so hasty. What you expect them Apache boys to do? They acted in self-defence, Sheriff. Agreed your folks had just suspicion to try to arrest 'em. But any fool knows they didn't attack that stage. Rattler took the diamonds and stuff from his father, who had received it from Koth-luni. I mean, his father was dead so he, you could say, was entitled to his property. Of course, he musta known where it came from and should have surrendered it, that's why, all in all, I think I've come to the right decision.'

'I don't like it,' Owens said, his frank, stone-grey eyes staring from his straight-boned features. 'You're going over my head. At least give me the two 'paches. Some-body's gotta git hanged.'

'I admire your eagerness to impose the full effects of civil law, Sheriff,' Hentig said, topping up his glass, 'but I've had another idea. Maybe a compromise.'

'Whadda ye mean, a compromise?'

'Well, look at it this way, Perry. Maybe we can celebrate? Old Geronimo and his band have finally surrendered after all these years. Or can we? Kothluni and his cut-throats are still out there and you and me, both, are going to be in deep trouble if we don't bring him in. General Miles and the Eastern Press are howling for this territory to be pacified once and for all. They don't want to hear about Kothluni and his savages raping, robbing, killing, burning, because that's what they're gonna go on doing. You and me know that trying to catch them is like trying to catch water in a sieve.'

'So?' Owens sniffed at his third glass. 'What are you saying?'

'I say we give Rattler and his two *compadres* the chance of going out and gittin' Kothluni. They're the best three scouts I got. If they succeed, they go free; if they fail, they go to the dungeons of Florida to serve their sentences.'

'Sir, I strongly object.' Lt Prendergast had been sitting at an adjacent desk attempting to work at a new-fangled Remington type-writer, tap-tapping away. Now, he jumped up, agitated, clicking his boot-heels. 'This flies in the face of all proper military procedure. Those men have already been sentenced.'

'Who's he?' Perry Owens asked, eyeing the fresh-faced, blond-haired youth. 'Who told him to shove his nose in?'

'Ah, this is my new adjutant, Giles Prendergast. I should have introduced you. His father, Colonel Prendergast, took up an important role in the Shenandoah cam-paign. Lost a leg. You may have heard of him?'

'No, cain't say I have. But what's this whipper-snapper know about anythang?'

'I'm a graduate of West Point. I know what is and what is not right.'

'Yeah, well, son, I'm a graduate of the Arizona frontier and I happen to think your captain knows a helluva lot more about Injin-fightin' than you do and he might jest have a germ of an idea.'

'I'm glad you see it that way, Perry. There's three good scouts. Why hang 'em or lock 'em up? That's a waste. I believe they can be useful.'

'But,' it occurred then to Prendergast, 'aren't you sentencing them to death, sending them out alone into Apache country?'

'They got two chances,' Owens said. 'They don't have to accept this mission.'

'They will,' Hentig smiled. 'And, with any luck, who knows? But, Lieutenant, I want you to keep this hush-hush. The sheriff's right. On the frontier you can't always fight by the book. You have to be prepared to bend the rules a bit. Now' – he went to his cupboard – 'how about a couple of bottles for you, Sheriff?'

Six

When they reached the railroad in their iron cage they saw about forty captive Apaches huddled in the dust and flints beside the track. Most were the remnants of Geronimo's band, their faces sullen masks, disarmed and defeated. For thirty years they had brought terror to the frontier and evaded US troops in the field. It hardly seemed possible that a few like this could have caused such fearful bloodshed, disrupted trade and cost the army and settlers millions of dollars. They had been promised they could return to the San Carlos reservation, which was bad enough, a barren tract ravaged by sandstorms, a prison camp in their own land, but instead they were being deported in chains. Some Rattler recognized who had taken no part in the war. There were Goth-kli, Ki-eh-Tah, and Toklani, who had served as army scouts. And Chaco, a friend of the white man, who had always spoken out against the hotheads who abandoned the reservation.

'Hang on, Sarge,' Rattler said, gripping McMullan's sleeve. 'What are these men doing here? They ain't hostiles. Never have been.'

'Git your hands off me.' The pot-bellied sergeant knocked away his arm with his carbine. 'Join the line. Git on the ground.'

'It's true what I say, McMullan. This isn't fair to these men.' Rattler stood his ground and pointed to the 'friendlies' he knew. 'They been our allies. Does the cap' know about this?'

'My orders is to round up every filthy savage of fighting age on the frontier and ship 'em to Florida.' McMullan's navy-blue shoddy blouse was ballooned taut by his gut, soaked with patches of sweat. 'General Miles has got the right idea in my opinion. Ye all oughta be shot.'

'I ain't no 'pache,' Rattler said, as he was escorted over from the cage to join the line. 'But this ain't right.'

'You sure look like one with that long hair and shifty eyes. Git sat in line.'

'Hey, Sarge.' Rattler lowered his voice. 'Ain't the cap'n told you?'

'Sure, I've been told about this crazy scheme. I'll tip ye the wink when it's time to make ya break.' McMullan gave him a gappy grin. 'You better run fast, boy, 'cause were gonna be shootin' at ye.'

'The rest of the men know?'

'No. They're gonna be shootin' to kill.' McMullan jabbed the barrel of his Spencer seven-shot carbine hard into Rattler's abdomen, knocking him down onto the track, raising his voice to growl, 'Git down, you heathen. You ain't got a chance in hell.'

Johnny Rattler sprawled, rubbing the pain away and looked along at the boxcars. There was no sign of old Geronimo and he presumed he had already been loaded. There were cries of outrage as other Indians were forced into an overcrowded boxcar and the door slammed tight. 'Follow me, boys, when I go,' he gritted out to his two scouts.

Sgt McMullan stamped along the track shouting at the blacksmith, 'Come on, get those irons on. What you hanging about for?'

The blacksmith was working slowly, his brain numbed by the noon-day heat of 120 degrees on Daniel Fahrenheit's scale. He was getting implacably closer. Only a few more prisoners to be chained. The bluecoats were busy pummelling the reluctant warriors into the second cattle truck. Up front, the big iron engine was snorting and blowing, getting up steam as if impatient to be away.

Sgt McMullan's boots came crunching back down the track. 'All right ye spalpeens,' he whispered, gutturally. 'Now's your chance.'

'Good.' Johnny Rattler grabbed the Spencer, twisting it from the sergeant's startled grip, bringing the butt up to crack against McMullan's jaw, sending him tumbling back down the gritty slope. 'Come on.'

Blue Owl and Seven Clouds didn't need any prompting. They sprang to a crouch, fast as rats up a drainpipe, following Rattler who had dived beneath the train and out the other side. They went springing towards an island of rocks in the scrub as they heard shouts behind them.

'There they are!' A guard was taking aim with his rifle behind them. A searing pain sliced through Rattler's forearm, and it began to sluice blood. He crouched low and began to weave and bob, zig-zagging from side to side, as more shots rang out and bullets zipped past his ears like angry bees.

'Damnation!' the guard cried. 'Why don't he run straight?'

The troopers had scrambled through beneath the train to join him and began blazing away, but the three escapees, jumping and bobbing like jack-rabbits, were fast making their way through the yucca and cactus ... 100 ... 200 ... 300 yards away ... almost out of accurate carbine range. They were scrambling up to the peak of the big pile of rocks and Rattler turned, poised at the top, transferred his Spencer to his left fist and raised it in triumph. A fool thing to do for a bullet nearly took off his ear. He went leaping away along the outcrop following his two *compadres*.

Sgt McMullan was back on his feet and bellowing, 'You six men, git on your hosses and follow me. You others, keep an eye on the prisoners. If they make a move shoot them down like dogs.'

He groaned as he waggled at his pained jaw and spat blood. He hauled himself with difficulty up onto his old army plug, drew his revolver, and led the six troopers out at a gallop. 'Shoot to kill,' he shouted. 'They cain't git far.'

The troopers followed him with a rattle of bridles and sabres, whooping as if on a fox hunt. They spurred their horses to a gallop weaving through the rocks.

Rattler and the two Apaches ran along the high ridge of rocks, avoiding the spikes and thorns and hooks of the cactus with innate grace, leaping across almost vertical rocks, from one to the other, landing on the balls of their feet and springing away. If they stayed on the high ground the horses would be unable to follow. When they reached the rim of the butte they doubled-back along one of its spurs to try to throw their pursuers off their track.

'Here!' Rattler called, and dived into a thick patch of prickly pear for cover. The two scouts followed him, crouched low, squeezing through the scratching spikes, their faces adamant, ignoring the needles, which would have made any other men cry out with pain. Rattler lay breathing hard and studied the cut in his arm. He could not help but feel sickened. Nobody likes the sight of his own blood flowing away. It was bad. Deep. But at least the bullet had cut clean through. He pulled his scout's scarlet bandanna from his forehead and wrapped it tight around the wound. Seven Clouds knelt to tie it tight for him. He took a whipcord wampum string from around his own neck, and tightened it around Rattler's upper arm as a tourniquet.

The troopers had gone around the head of the mesa of rocks and were riding back. Rattler could hear the jingle of their harness, smell the sweat of their horses. It sounded as if they were dismounting, climbing up the rocks towards them. He nodded at the Apaches and hissed, 'Stay down.'

The troopers came stumbling and cursing, slashing their sabres into the cactus thickets, clambering along the top of the mesa. 'I'm gonna kill the bastards,' one screamed. Rattler was sure he would have liked to, but he went on past.

Another heavier, trooper came crunching along behind them. 'Keep ya eyes peeled, boys. They could be anywhere.' It was Sgt McMullan's voice. His boots were only a foot from Blue Owl's nose. The former scout mischievously grabbed his boot in a fulcrum lock and sent him crashing face forward into the cactus. McMullan howled and cursed as he extricated himself. Rattler poked the Spencer through the under-growth at him and hissed, 'Howdy, Sarge. Don't say nuthin'. The cap' won't like it.'

The other troopers had turned and one yelled, 'What's wrong? You see something?'

McMullan looked about ready to have an apoplexy as he picked thorns from his face. For moments Rattler thought he would give them away. 'No,' McMullan bellowed. 'I tripped, thassall. Come on, we're wasting time. Let's git back to the train.'

Rattler waited until he heard them return to their horses and move away before crawling out. His arm had begun to throb. Not a good start, but at least they were free. He looked across the heat-hazed chasms and saw a spiral of dust where the troopers were picking their way back through the pin-cushion of desert plants. He heard the harsh panting of the locomotive as it slowly moved away. Those poor devils, some of the last warriors of a once proud and mighty nation, being taken away to incarceration in a strange land.

'Thass where we gotta go, boys,' he muttered, looking across to the blue haze of the Chiracahua Mountains rising high in the distance. 'Kothluni's out there somewhere. But I ain't sure he's gonna be pleased to see us.'

They ran on across the wilderness at a steady pace all afternoon until the great red ball of sun began to sink behind the distant barrancas, bathing their precipitous walls pink and blue, sinking away into a glorious inferno.

They must have run for twenty miles or so. Running did not bother the two Apache boys, although they would have preferred to be on horseback. They were fit and lithe and could have gone on another thirty. But the pumping of his heart was making Rattler lose much blood. He felt sick and light-headed and began to miss his step and stumble. His right hand had gone numb, taken on a blue pallor, but if he released the tourniquet the wound began to flow again.

'It's no good, boys. I'm gonna have ta rest up,' he gasped out. 'We must be near the San Carlos reservation. Ain't your mother got a hogan there, Seven Clouds?'

'Sure.' Seven Clouds nodded, seriously. 'She good medicine woman. She know what to do.'

'Luckily that shot didn't crack the bone.' He studied the fly-buzzing cut with an expression of disgust. 'But if this turns gangrenous I'm gonna end up worse than a one-armed no-good savage. Damn that McMullan. He's got a grudge 'ginst me.'

Blue Owl had found a forked stick which he carried as some sort of weapon. When he leapt over a rock he nearly landed on a coiled rattlesnake that had come out of his hole to hunt in the night. It raised itself, its fangs bared, its tail rattling, sinisterly, its heat-seeking mechanism enabling the short-sighted reptile to target the man. Blue Owl dodged to one side and pinned the side-winder down by its head with the stick, grabbing at its tail with his free hand. Seven Clouds came to his help, slashing the creature's throat with a sharp flint.

Johnny Rattler sank back against a stone to rest. He took a tin of phosphorous strikes from his jacket pocket and tossed them across. 'A snake is a steak, eh, boys?' He tried to force a grin. 'Let's eat.'

Seven Clouds made a small fire of mesquite twigs while Blue Owl skinned the snake, and they roasted the flesh and chewed on it as darkness closed in. 'Waal, all I can say is it's better than bein' cooped up in one of them damn goods vans,' Rattler said, but he felt sick and his mind was wavering, and when he lay back he suddenly passed out into a black unconsciousness.

When he awoke he was in a low-roofed hogan, bathed in sweat, lying on a bed of skins as an old Indian woman made signs in the dust and moaned magic words over him as she dusted his face with a bunch of strange-smelling feathers. He recognized the dark-grooved face of Seven Clouds' mother.

'How long I been out?' he muttered.

'Not long,' Blue Owl replied. 'I hump you here on my back.'

In the semi-darkness of this lean-to among the rocks, lit only by a fire's glow, Rattler saw a young Indian girl sat cross-legged, a blanket around her head and shoulders. It was Seven Clouds' sister, Ekinata, her bronzed face smooth and oval, unlined as yet by work and worry. She wore a patterned blouse and voluminous skirts over buckskin leggings. Rattler had been a guest at her initiation ceremony two years before. He remembered her in her best buckskin dress, her cheeks painted with yellow pollen, dancing through the night as the tribe chanted and feasted and prayed that she would be a good woman. The Apache put great stock on female virtue.

'Hiya,' he smiled. 'How's it going?'

'Your wound will heal soon,' she replied, shyly. 'Mother has put the juice of the geeya flower on it. It sets hard like a gum and stops the blood flow. The poultice of herbs and the magic will help, too.'

'Yeah? Thanks,' he muttered. 'I guess I gotta try an' believe in that ol' black magic if I'm gonna be a 'pache again.'

Ekinata passed him a gourd of water. 'You need to drink.'

He lay and studied the girl as the others talked and smoked. How different she was, in her gentle ways, in spite of the tough life she led, to that catlike, crazy Mex harlot, Conchita, or the soft-skinned, cherubic-faced Pearl Holm, who seemed to have led a cosseted life compared to the other two.

Seven Clouds was talking bitterly about the near-starvation conditions on the reservation and the cruelty of Mean Man.

Mean Man was The People's name for Frank Tiffany, the agent in charge. It was well-known that he cheated and stole from them, refused to give them their due provisions, and would not allow them to leave the reservation to hunt.

'We like to give you food but we nothing,' the mother said. 'We get one cupful flour a week. If any of The People protest he lock them up in jailhouse. Some boys been months locked up in there. Now they kill our sons, take our men away, we starve. What can we do?'

Rattler shook his head, sadly. There was nothing he could say.

Mother and daughter helped him to his feet and, making sure the coast was clear, took him to a small cave on the hillside, shielding the entrance with sage brush.

Seven Clouds and Blue Owl settled down beside him to sleep. 'Nobody find us here,' Blue Owl grunted.

'We hope,' Rattler said.

Seven

Maybe life tasted sour to some, but there
was jubilation in Tombstone that Geronimo
and his Apaches had at last been enchained
and deported. The days of terror and fire
must surely soon be over. Now men could
go out to their mines in the hills in safety
without fear of attack.

In Morgan and Vine's saloon a sometime
rustler and horse thief, Sam Cook, watched
the dancing and singing, the clamour of
drinking with a twitchy smile on his lips. He
was a thin-faced man in a tall Stetson and
tattered riding duster. Like most of the others
he had a heavy revolver stuck in his belt.

'Them bucks they took away musta left
plenty of ponies around,' he opined as he
leaned on the bar between two cronies.
'How about we ride up there and get our-

selves a herd?'

'Yeah, I allus wanted to git me a Chiracahua scalp.' Jimmy O'Farrel was a whiskey-breath brawler who had gotten his nose bitten off in a fight. A steel plate covered the empty socket. 'It's time we give them redskins a whaling.'

Jed Thomas was a down-on-his-luck smalltime mugger and ne'er-do-well, attired in a dirt-brown derby and shabby frock coat. He wasn't too sure. A month before he wouldn't have dared to venture far into the hills. But with most of the warriors taken away it couldn't be too dangerous. He was easily led. 'I'm game,' he muttered.

The threesome left the saloon, unhitched their horses, and rode out of town heading up the San Pedro valley towards the San Carlos. After hours of riding, they reached the upper valley, and saw the start of the reservation, the wickiups, hogans and shacks dotted at intervals across the rough ground. One of the first hogans was that of Jack Seven Clouds' mother and beyond that was a thorn corral with a herd of half-wild paint horses milling about.

'Let's git 'em, boys,' Cook whooped, wielding his lariat and galloping towards the corral.

Johnny Rattler was woken from his haze of feverish sleep by the sound of shooting. 'What'n hell is going on?' He crawled to the mouth of the cave, McMullan's Spencer carbine in his left hand. Three men were blamming their revolvers, opening the gate of the corral and making off with the Indians' herd. At that moment an Apache boy ran out from one of the shacks, knife in hand, running to fight them. The horsemen surrounded him, whupping him with their lariats until he fell down whimpering, covering his head.

Rattler recognized the horse thief, Sam Cook, by his tall hat and long duster coat. He had pulled a knife from his pocket and jumped down to stand over the boy. It looked like he was about ready to take his hair.

'Hang on, boys,' he said, holding back the two scouts, who crowded the entrance beside him. 'We don't wanna git involved in this.'

Cook had been distracted by the howl of the raiders who had spotted a young girl in buckskin leggings beneath her skirts break from the rocks and go sprinting for cover. It was Ekinata. The other two horsemen were almost upon her. An ugly character, with a steel noseplate, was whirling his lariat. He roped her and brought her tumbling down. He slithered from his horse yelling, 'She's mine, boys. I'm first.'

Ekinata kicked and screamed and begged as the two men held her down. 'Aw, hell,' Rattler groaned, and, in spite of the haziness in his head, and the wound in his forearm, raised the Spencer and squinted along the sights. His first shot cracked out and split the iron-nosed man's head like a water melon, splashing the girl with blood.

The shabby man in a brown derby, Jed Thomas, spun around, his face panicked, pulling out his revolver, searching for the source of the shot. Before he could fire a slug ploughed through his chest, tumbling him onto his back to lie prostrate in the dust.

Cook wasn't waiting to argue; he leaped into his saddle, spurred his horse away, hanging low over its mane, heading back the way he had come. As he passed the cave, Rattler carefully took him out and Cook threw up his hands, catapulting backwards into the rocks.

'Whew!' Johnny Rattler gave a whistle of relief 'Got the varmints. That settled their hash. But it ain't gonna look too good when it gets out.'

'We go git their hosses, their guns,' Blue Owl said pushing past him and bounding down the slope.

'Thanks, Johnny.' Jack Seven Clouds patted his shoulder. 'I owe you my sister's life. Nice shooting.'

'Yeah, it weren't too bad, was it?' Rattler smiled, as he hobbled down behind them.

'Seeing as I ain't feeling a hundred per cent.'

He walked over to Ekinata, who was lying on the ground, her eyes squeezed closed, her face petrified by fear. He knelt and smoothed her hair, straightened her skirt. 'It's OK,' he said, huskily. 'Them fellas ain't gonna hurt you. They ain't gonna hurt nobody no more.'

A shot barrelled out from the hillside and spat into the dust by his moccasin boot. Rattler looked up and saw a dark crowlike figure in a straight-brimmed black hat and frock coat sitting a horse on a ridge looking down at them. It was Mean Man Tiffany. On either side were two Indian police in their high-bowled hats and navy pea-jackets and one of them was levering his carbine. Rattler rolled behind a rock. 'Keep your head down,' he yelled to Ekinata.

Another slug whistled past his head, chiselling rock. He rested the Spencer on a ledge and took aim. The Indian agent spun his horse around with alarm. Rattler released another three shots in rapid succession as the reservation guards hurriedly took cover. Seven Clouds and Blue Owl had leaped onto two of the dead horse-thieves' mustangs and were galloping towards him, leading the third. Rattler jumped up, tossed the Spencer to Seven Clouds, and swung, with some difficulty, due to his arm, up into the saddle. He whirled the horse and grinned at Ekinata. 'Take care of yourself. Or try to.'

He kicked in his heels and the bronco raced away as he followed his two friends across the rough terrain, his long hair blowing across his face. 'Yeehaugh!' he shouted. 'Let's go!'

When they reached the ridge at the end of the reservation he looked back, but there was no sign of Tiffany or his two traitorous police. 'The cowards have gone back to the safety of the agency jail, I reckon,' he grinned. 'But I got a feelin' we're gonna meet again one day.'

Captain George Hentig was in a foul mood. He had had a cursory message over the wire from General Miles to attend a meeting at Tucson ... TO EXPLAIN YOUR ACTIONS. It had meant him riding for three days and overnight with a platoon of men down from Fort Bowie in the hills the 105 miles to Tucson and a hard journey through a dust blizzard to be in time for the appointment. He hardly had time to grab a bowl of coffee in the garrison, or to brush down his uniform before being ushered into the general's presence. He saluted and glanced at the officers sitting around a table. They were all younger and of higher rank with unfamiliar faces.

'So, what's going on, Captain?' Miles grunted, gutturally, when Hentig was seated opposite him. 'First you let three convicted murderers escape custody. And now this' – he pushed a copy of that morning's *Tucson Citizen* across to him.

Hentig saw with some surprise, the glaring headlines, GUNFIGHT AT THE SAN

CARLOS – THREE WHITE MEN KILLED ON RESERVATION. He picked it up, found his spectacles, and read it through, his face as thunderous as the general's.

'I suppose this is all part of your so-called plan to bring Kothluni in? Have you given your Apache scouts *carte blanche* to shoot down whomsoever they please?'

'Well,' Hentig replied, 'it looks like they're doing humanity a service. They're culling a few of the frontier scum.'

'What, man?' Nelson Miles roared. 'What kind of answer is that?'

'Might I draw your attention to the editorial, sir, in the column alongside? It seems a balanced judgement.' And Hentig began to read it out, 'While by no means condoning the actions of the three renegade soldiers it is in some ways fortunate that they were at the reservation at the time. The settlers in the vicinity have for too long been left to suffer from the rash acts of such senseless and cowardly ruffians like Cook,

114

O'Farrel and Thomas, who thought they could line their pockets and gain a little cheap notoriety by attacking a few peaceable Indian women and boys. Why, we might ask, does not agent Tiffany take better care and give protection to those in his charge?'

'We can read, Hentig.' Miles was a general of a different ilk to General Crook. He was a military man of thunder and iron, with little sympathy for liberal sentiments on the Indian question. He was probably one of Sheridan's school, which advocated a policy of total genocide. 'I asked you a question - was this part of your plan?'

'No, it wasn't. I have sent out these three men under cover, to ingratiate themselves with Kothluni and either bring him in or lead us to him.' Captain Hentig finished reading and put his spectacles away. 'It looks like they got caught in some kinda crossfire here. But let's look at the bright side, it should give Kothluni good cause to believe they're renegades and on his side.'

'What makes you think they won't be on his side now you've let them get away scot free? Or heading for the border? Are you soft in the head, man?'

'No, I ain't, General. I would trust those three scouts with my life. I've promised them their freedom if they succeed. I ask that you honour that pact.'

'Give my word to three murdering Apaches?' Miles roared. 'Are you crazy, man?'

'General, I don't take kindly to words like that. Two of them are law-abiding Apaches who hate that torturing fiend Kothluni as much as you or I do. Their leader Sergeant John Rattler, has a touch of Yaqui blood, was brought up for awhile in Kothluni's band, but, yes, he's a boy I trust.'

'Pah! Trust! I'd rather trust a real rattler,' Miles snorted, as his officers murmured their amusement. 'So, Hentig, you sit on your backside and send out three scouts to do your work?'

'Look, General,' Hentig sighed, pointing a

116

finger to a map of Arizona Territory on the wall. 'I don't know whether you're aware we've had to keep the lid on an Apache area the size of France and Germany combined these past thirty years. Now we've got the last few hostiles bottled up in the south-east corner of the frontier, the Chiricahuas, but it's still like looking for a needle in a haystack. Kothluni's as crafty as a fox. He could pop up anywhere. That's why I've backed this undercover operation.'

'Might I remind *you*, sir, I'm in charge of the operations in this Territory,' Miles bristled. 'You presume too much.'

'Yeah, well, maybe,' Hentig growled. 'And maybe I'm counting the days to my retirement. I'd hoped to see the Territory at peace and prosperous before then. Might I say while I'm here that I protest at the way we've been ordered to send loyal scouts off to the dungeons with Geronimo's gang. It's a sad day. It seems like there ain't no such thing as honour in this man's army any more.'

'Good God!' one of the officers, a major of infantry, exclaimed, expressing the shock of the others that Hentig should speak to the general in this way.

General Miles sat and glowered at the company for a while, got to his feet and went over to a cabinet, opening a bottle of bourbon. 'War's a different kettle of fish these days. There's no such thing as trust. Come on, George, have a glass. Might soothe your tender feelings. I'm going to give your plan a chance before I move my men in.' He turned to his officers and grinned, slapping Hentig on the shoulder. 'We have to excuse these old war horses. They've got some odd ideas about honouring the enemy out here on the frontier. If your boys pull this off, George, I'll see they get what they deserve.'

Captain Hentig got stiffly to his feet and accepted the glass. 'Reinstatment as scouts?'

'Yes, sure, anything you want,' Miles soothed. 'I see now why you've never made more than captain. You're too hot-headed and outspoken for your own good. Cheers, Hentig. Down the hatch.'

'Cheers, General.'

Maybe, Captain Hentig thought, Miles wasn't as bad as he was painted. But he was glad he had got what he believed off his chest.

Eight

They had ammunition for Sam Cook's big old .45 Colt Frontier, for Tin Nose O'Farrel's Smith & Wesson .44 and Thomas's antiquated .38 which the horse-thieves had been carrying with them, but Rattler had spent the seven slugs of the trusty Spencer carbine and wanted to re-stock. 'Hang on, boys,' he shouted as they rode. 'We ain't far from Globe. You two make camp here. I got an idea where I can get me some bullets. And maybe some grub.'

The two Apaches nodded, mutely. They had grown used to their sergeant – or former sergeant – dashing off on some spur-of-the-moment notice. Night was coming on, so they settled down, loose-hitched their new horses and let them seek whatever nourishment they could among the thorns.

The mining town of Globe was not very far from the San Carlos reservation. It was getting late by the time Johnny Rattler rode along the curving main street. Most hard-working folks had gone to their beds, but there were a few drinkers and card-players in McGinty's Saloon, its interior lit by flickering oil lamps, as Rattler went clopping by.

Holm's General Goods Emporium, which sold practically everything from buttons to buggies, was shuttered, and the rooms above the store appeared to be in darkness. In fact, as he sat his horse Rattler could hear two separate snorings, rising and falling in harmony, drifting from the open window. He grinned and rode his horse around the back of the clapboard building. One window was lit by flickering candlelight so he gave a low whistle through his teeth. There was no response. He took a coin and flicked it up through the open window to drop rattling on the floor inside. He couldn't be sure, but he hoped he'd got the right room.

Yes. Pearl Holm's quizzical face peered from the window. Her hair was tied in rag curlers and she was holding her hands across her naked breasts. She eyed the handsome young quarter-breed with wide-eyed surprise. 'Johnny!' she cried in a stage whisper. 'What'n hell you doin' here?'

'Lookin' fer you.'

'What you mean?' she said, hoarsely. 'You come to give me a ride agin?'

'Waal.' He flashed a smile up at her. 'Not exactly.'

'You got a nerve. Ain't you seen the paper 'bout that shoot-out at the San Carlos? There's been a posse out lookin' fer you all day.'

'Yeah, we figured it best to lead 'em a dance and let 'em git on with their lookin' 'fore we make a break for the hills. So, Pearl, how are you?'

'Oh, you know. The same ol' thang. Workin' in the store all day. Stuck in here all night. Look at that moon, Johnny. Ain't it beautiful? I wish I could be like you, ride free, do what'n hell I liked. It jest ain't fair bein' a gal.'

'Yeah?' Johnny looked up at the great translucent globe rising beyond the cold grey mountains. 'It's a night made for love, ain't it, gal?'

'You can say that agin, Johnny,' she said, and bunched her breasts up so the nipples nearly spilled over her forearms and he could get a good view as she hung out the window. 'Why doncha come up?'

'What about your ma and pa? Or is it them I could hear snoring?'

'You said it, Johnny. They're dead to the world,' she half-whispered. 'Jeeze, they sure git on a gal's nerves.'

'To tell you the truth, Pearl, I was wondering if you stock ammo for a Spencer carbine? And we could do with some vittles.'

Pearl gave a snort of dismay. 'Huh! An' I thought you'd come callin' to see me.'

'I sure have, Pearl,' Rattler smiled. 'I been

thinkin' about ya. I missed ya. But a man can call for two separate reasons, cain't he?'

'Oh, you! Why do I like you? You're jest gonna end up gittin' yourself killed. You're dang fool crazy. If my folks knew I was even talkin' to ya they'd have a fit.'

'In that case...' Rattler agilely jumped up to balance on his saddle and leapt for a bough of the big cottonwood in the yard swinging himself up like a circus trapeze artiste, jumping from one bough to the next to her bedroom window, stepping neatly inside. 'Howdy, Pearl.' He held her in his arms, his fingers sweeping down the flow of her bare spine to her soft and ample buttocks, slipping inside her calico pantalettes. 'Waal, whadda ya know?'

'Jeez, Johnny.' Her lips were open moistly against his mouth, her head seemingly spinning. 'Wait 'til I git these rags outa my hair. I must look a sight.'

'I ain't lookin' at ya hair, Pearl.'

'Aw, gee. I was just about to git into my

nightie.' Pearl tried to fluff up her frizzy fair hair. 'You got me in a tizz. Whadda ya do to a gal, Johnny?'

'Whadda ya want me to do, Pearl?' His head had slipped down to kiss her breasts, playing the nipples with his teeth, gently easing her down onto her bed burying his face in the soft mounds. 'Holy Jehosophat, you're a vision of heaven. An angel. You're beautiful.'

'Shush!' She froze, gripping hold of him tight. 'What's that?'

He, too, had heard the sound of somebody or something thumping heavily against the bedroom door. And then there was a snuffling at the crack between door and floor.

'Satan,' Pearl hissed. 'Go away.'

'Satan?'

'Yes,' she giggled. 'We call him that 'cause he's black as pitch and allus pees on people he don't like.'

There was a squirting sound and dog's urine trickled beneath the door.

'Looks like he don't like me,' Rattler grinned.

'Don't be sceered. He won't bite ya. Ouch! And don't you, neither.'

'I'm sorry, Pearl. You're gittin' me excited.'

'Yes, I can feel that.' She was unbuttoning his rough serge jacket and pulling it from his bare bronzed body. 'You're gittin' me that way, too.'

'Maybe we better stop?' He rested on his elbows, his dark, glowing eyes, amid his long black fronds of hair, studying her. 'I don't wancha to do nuthin' you don't wanna do, Pearl.'

'It's OK,' she whispered, clutching fingers into his hair and pulling his lips down to hers. 'I ain't a virgin. That Jim Doogan did it to me when I was thirteen. He got me in the barn down at the corral. The great lummox. I couldn't stop him. But I ain't done it with nobody since, I swear. I been waiting for the right one.'

'You reckon that's me?' he asked, huskily.

'Sure I do. There ain't no doubt in my

mind. I've been longing to see you again.'

With that they began kissing and grabbing at each other like a frenzy had come over them, as if each wanted to be one and part of the other, as if some great tidal wave had hit them and was sweeping them on. Somewhere at the back of her mind Pearl could hear the iron bed's headrail rattling rhythmically against the planks of the bedroom wall, the springs grating and groaning.

'Shush!' she cried. 'They'll hear us. We'll wake 'em.' But somehow she didn't care and gripped him tighter, cleaved by his force, his virility as on and on they strove...

'Jeez, Johnny,' she sighed after a strenuous half-hour, her breasts making a sucking sound as they parted from his chest and he raised himself above her. 'You sure know how to pleasure a gal. I ain't never been done like that afore.'

'Yeah?' he smiled at her and lay back. 'You ain't so bad yourself, Pearl, fer a beginner.'

'What you gonna do, Johnny?' she asked some while later, snuggling up to him.

'Where you gonna go?'

He wiped sweat from his strong neck and stared at the ceiling, listening, but all was quiet, apart from the parental snores. 'Can you keep a secret, Pearl? This is real hush-hush.'

'Sure I can, Johnny Rattler. Cross my heart hope to die.'

'I'm on a mission for the army. The cap's promised I can go free if I can bring Koth-luni in, or his scalp.'

'Kothluni!' Pearl gave an involuntary shudder. 'But nobody can catch Kothluni. That fiend! They say he's got some kinda power protects him.'

'Yeah? Well so have I. You know, I've had an idea, Pearl. I gotta try to keep in contact with the cap – Cap'n Hentig up at Fort Bowie. Maybe you could help?'

'How so, Johnny?'

'You wanna see me agin, doncha?'

'Sure I do. I can't wait. I'll do anything you want.'

'Waal, if I git a chance I'll visit you some

night. Maybe soon. Maybe not for a while. An' the next morning you can send a message over the telegraph wire to Fort Bowie. My code name's The Eagle.'

'The Eagle? Hey, that suits you more than Rattler. Ain't this excitin', Johnny?'

'Yeah, it sure does suit me. I swoop and pounce.'

He grabbed at her so she almost screamed, clutching her mouth as she watched him swing out of the small bed. 'There's a water jug there you can use,' she said.

'How about them bullets?' he asked, as he did so.

'Sure, follow me.' She unlocked the door, and tried to quieten the big black dog as he jumped up at her. 'Down, boy.' She lit a candle in a holder, put her finger to her lips and beckoned Rattler. 'Get off,' he growled as Satan urinated on his leg.

'Who's that?' a voice called out from her mother's bedroom. 'Is that you, Pearl?'

'Yes, I'm just going out to the privy. I gotta go.'

'Lock the door when you come back in.'

There was a creaking of bedsprings and a groan, and Pearl grinned at him. 'Come on,' she hissed.

The boards creaked, too, as they climbed down a narrow staircase to the shop. There was a sweet, musty smell of barrels of apples and nuts, mingled with paraffin and slabs of salt bacon hung on hooks from the rafters, the scent of the saddle leather, soap, molasses, with all around the orderly jumble of a general store.

'Here.' Pearl led him through it, a shawl around her shoulders, her comely buttocks swinging in the loose pantalettes. She reached into a cabinet and produced a cardboard box of bullets. 'Let's see. What did you say, .53 calibre? That's it. How many can I do you for, sir?'

'Make it five boxes, miss. I might be pretty busy.'

'Five boxes at twelve dollars a box. Shall I put it on your account, sir?'

'Yeah, an' how about a hunk of that

bacon? And some cooking beans. And coffee beans. And, let's see, some of this candy. I gotta keep the boys happy.'

'Why not take some for Kothluni, too, as a sweetener? And some chawin' baccy? And some of these cheap necklaces? Ain't that the sorta stuff Injins like?'

'Aincha got any whiskey? Thass more to his taste.'

'No, sorry, sir. We don't stock it.' Pearl was busy wrapping his purchases. 'How about one of these nice shirts for yourself? Finest plaid. This black and blue one'll suit you nice. Won't show the dirt. Keep you warm at night. Don't want you catching cold.'

'Yeah.' Rattler tried on the shirt, admired himself in a glass. He picked a black low-crowned Stetson from a pile, pulled it over his brow at a jaunty angle. 'Mighty fine, gal. How much I owe you?'

'Aw, thass OK.'

'No. Don't want you gittin' into trouble.' He took a roll of bills from his pocket, peeled several greasy greenbacks and tossed them down. 'Courtesy of the late Sam Cook, you might say.'

Pearl totted up the reckoning and gave him change from the till. She unbolted the side door and hung onto his waist as he slipped past. 'Johnny, take care. I'm sceered you ain't nevuh gonna come back. Them Apache devils! Do ya have to go after them? Cain't you take me with you? We could cross the frontier, make a new life in Mexico.'

'Thass a nice idea, Pearl, but I can't.' He kissed her, tenderly. 'I gotta do this. I've given my word to the Cap.'

'Johnny, please—'

But he had sprung away into the darkness and with one leap was on his mustang, pulling its reins free and swirling it around. 'So long, *muchacha*. And thanks.'

With that he went pounding away through the night, riding from the huddle of houses, heading out into the harsh, moonstreaked mountains, not looking back.

They saw the smoke after two days' horse

travel. It was roiling up through the summer-still air from a canyon of the high Chiracahua Mountains. The smoke from a greenwood fire, broken into small clouds by the sender's blanket, asked, 'Who are you?'

Rattler reined in his mustang and sat for a few moments watching. The smoke was half-a-day's ride away but he knew that whoever sent it would be waiting, watching. He jumped from his mount, took Tin Nose's wide-bladed Bowie from his belt and flashed a reply off the sun; 'Rattler ... Blue Owl ... Seven Clouds. We have killed many white men. They hunt us.'

The Indians had developed a smoke and sun flashing language as subtle and many-worded as their inter-tribal sign-language which had been learned by Rattler during his stay with Kothluni's people. He watched for a reply and sure enough it came drifting up into the sky: 'We are in the narrow gorge where the water runs fast and the grass is green.'

'We know the place,' Rattler flashed with

the blade. 'We will come. We will talk.'

'Come,' the smoke replied lazily.

'They will either talk or they will kill us, boys. That's the risk we gotta take.'

'We kill Kothluni?' Blue Owl grunted.

'Nope. That's too risky. We'd never get outa this country with our hair. We gotta play him along, ask his protection, pretend to be friends, wait our chance to lead him into ambush.'

'He will look into our eyes and know we are lying,' Jack Seven Clouds said, a wince of fear on his dark face. 'You cannot trick Kothluni. He will give us the long lingering death.'

'No, we can play it right, boys,' Rattler said. 'Kothluni needs us as much as we need him. Come on. *Andale!*'

He nudged his mustang with his moccasined heels, putting the scrubby horse to a canter that would cover the rough climb at a good pace without exhausting him. It was hot hard work for a man and harder for the animal beneath him. All about them the land was rugged limbs of red and brown rock leading down from the mountains, a vast emptiness known only to the Apache and a few intrepid troopers or scalphunters who ventured into it. It was bakehouse hot, so hot it rasped into a man's lungs. The only vegetation was the spiky barrel cactus and saguaro which stood with their arms raised as if warning them. Rattler sucked on a pebble to bring some saliva to his dry mouth and urged his horse on, eager to reach *El Cañon de Agua* – where the smoke was coming from. There would be green grass there for their broncs. And, in some ways, he was eager to pit his wits against the crafty Kothluni. He felt at home here.

He did not want to reach the canyon in darkness. He preferred to meet the Apache in daylight when there would be more chance of winning their confidence. So, as night came on they camped in a defile of the rocks. They fed the horses a little grain from a sack slung from Blue Owl's saddle, and gave them most of the water in their wooden canteens. They saved a few sips for themselves, but in country like this the horses came first.

They hobbled their mounts with rawhide lariats and, without making a fire, settled down and carved themselves strips of the salt bacon. They chewed on it raw sucking its nourishment, swallowing it down. The effect was to make them thirstier, but that was something an Apache learned to live with. Tomorrow there would be water. If they lived.

They hardly spoke, saving their breath, huddling in their blankets against the night cold, listening to the harsh screams of animals in the darkness, predators on the prowl, that other hunt eternal, the battle for survival, for life. And each man wondered in his heart if this expedition wasn't a fools' errand, whether tomorrow would be their last day on this earth.

But exhaustion kicked in and Rattler soon drifted into a troubled sleep. The screech of an owl woke him and he saw the sharp-beaked bird perched on a rock watching them. It was a bad omen. It was the cool of dawn when the beasts, the lizards, kangaroo rats, snakes, mice, even the more rare black panther, bear, and the great Gila monster, would be seeking a last meal before hiding all day in their underground dens. The time of day when the hawks and other desert birds were testing their wings, drifting on the thermals seeking any lizard or jack-rabbit that was foolish enough to venture out. It was a hard land. Rattler experienced a pit of dread in his stomach. Today was the testing time. Who would not know fear at the prospect of meeting Kothluni and his boys on their home ground? There would be three against about thirty warriors. The odds were not good.

'Come on, boys,' he called. 'Let's go.'

Nine

El Cañon de Agua was uncannily silent and seemingly deserted, the constant whispering of the wind at this high altitude being the only sound. But Rattler saw a mound of fresh pony dung in the grass and a cactus wren fly from a thornbush on the slope and knew they were not alone. They were being watched. The hair at his nape prickled, his heart pounded and sweat broke out on his palms. Now was the testing time. But such was his thirst he bounded from his horse, looked about him, fell down, cupped his hands and drank from the fast-flowing stream. An arrow almost parted his hair and thudded into the muddy bank. He froze for moments, remained on one knee, and turned around slowly. It was a good sign. They had not killed him yet. But perhaps they wanted to take their time?

The thin, dark-faced "savages" appeared from behind their rocks like ghosts, first one, then another, until there was a deathly encirclement of nearly forty carbines, lances, and arrows taut-strung in readiness aimed at the three former soldiers. Last to appear was Kothluni in his scarlet cloth turban. 'Lay your guns aside,' he shouted in Apache. 'Or you die.'

Rattler glanced at Blue Owl and Seven Clouds, slowly drew the Colt Frontier from his belt and tossed it onto the ground. His companions followed suit surrendering their revolvers.

'Send your horse away,' Kothluni commanded, his fierce eyes on the Spencer carbine in the saddle boot.

'Skit!' Rattler hissed, shooing the mustang to go drink further up the stream.

'And the knife.'

Rattler took the Bowie from its scabbard and thudded it into the ground by the arrow. 'We have come in friendship,' he shouted in words remembered from his boyhood. 'We have come to help you in your fight.'

To say that Kothluni was an ugly-looking varmint would be by way of an understatement. The Apache were not the most handsome of tribes to begin with. Beneath his ragged red headscarf Kothluni's face was a hollow-cheeked mask, his green eyes as cold as obsidian. If he grinned, which was seldom and generally when he was torturing some unfortunate captive, he revealed a set of broken and twisted fangs. Unlike other tribes, the True People did not go in much for bodily decoration, but Kothluni had four gold rings inserted in the cartilage of each ear, rings torn from the fingers of American or Mexican women.

He stepped down through the rocks and faced them, his lips pursed in a thin grim line. He was garbed in a baggy and torn white shirt, and a breechclout with its long tails fore and aft which revealed strongly muscled, sun-blackened thighs.

'So, you have come back to your people?'

he said, and his mouth split into a cruel grin. 'You fight alongside the Hairfaces against us for many years. Now you return as a friend?'

'That's the way it is,' Rattler said. 'We had no choice.' The other Apaches had closed in around them, thin, but leanly muscled, dark-skinned and naked except for moccasin boots and loin-cloths. Most wore their hair hanging to their shoulders but some had it tucked under head-coverings. One wore a battered cavalry hat with a feather stuck in the band. All eyed them with a suspicion akin to hatred. Their sharp-pointed arrows and lances bristled in readiness.

'You have no doubt heard what happened to us.' Rattler noticed an old Indian who had hung about the stables at Fort Bowie. 'You have your spies.'

'You were thrown out of the army for killing three *pinda-lik-oyi*.'

'Yes, white-eyes scum who tried to cheat us. Geronimo has been sent in chains to the dungeons of Florida, far, far away. They

141

wanted to send us, too, but we escaped. Then we killed three more *pinda-lik-oyi* filth who wanted to rob and rape the San Carlos Indian people. The Hairfaces sent a posse after us but we easily outpaced them because we know the Indian paths.'

'So, why do you come here? We do not want you among us. Why should we not make you suffer – truly suffer – for killing and imprisoning our people? How you like that, eh?'

'We did wrong to help the Hairfaces,' Blue Owl put in. 'But now we know how treacherous they are, that that is the way they would reward us, we have only hatred in our hearts for them. We intend to fight them to the end.'

'Ay-yai-yee!' One of the warriors gave a howl of anger and sprang forward, poking at Blue Owl with his lance. 'He lies. Give him to me. I will make him speak the truth before he dies.'

'Do not trust them, Kothluni,' another said.

'I trust no man,' the leader hissed, and stepped forward, staring into each of the captives' eyes. They met his gaze, barely flinching.

'I do not know if they speak the truth,' Kothluni said. 'But, on the other hand, it would seem they are outlaws. They need our help. As we need theirs. We need bullets. We' – he grinned craftily – 'could use some whiskey. I believe I will put them to a test.'

The warriors started shouting and squabbling, some protesting at this decision. The one in the cavalry hat stepped forward and slapped Jack Seven Clouds hard across the face. Jack held his head high, ignored him.

'Enough.' Kothluni raised his hand. 'We will give them a chance.'

'I have gifts for you,' Rattler said. 'I was a boy when I was among you. I am a man now. We will smoke in friendship.' He moved carefully to his horse and took the tobacco from his saddle-bags, raising it to show them. He pulled out the trinkets, the bracelets and necklaces. 'Give these to your squaws.'

Kothluni reached out a hand for the tobacco and said, 'Come. We have our camp further up the creek.'

As camps go, the Apaches did not go in for graceful living. A few temporary wickiups of mesquite branches and skins, some sullen flat-faced squaws in their blankets sat around their smoky cooking fires; some naked mop-headed brats; a few stunted ponies. They could up-sticks and be off at the first hint of attack. They would climb away separately across mountain paths to regroup at some other preordained camp. Nor did they use the stone pipe like other tribes. They rolled the tobacco in corn husks or dried leaves and passed the fat tube around. Sometimes they doctored it with the seeds of a plant grown by Mexicans which made them laugh, foolishly, and roll around. But it was not so good as the rot-gut whiskey which sent the braves berserk.

'You are the son of Tribollet,' Kothluni said. 'You get us whiskey.'

'To do that I need cash. Gold. The yellow stone.' He produced a handful of coins, silver dollars and a golden eagle, worth twenty. 'This sorta stuff.'

'You got gold there'. Kothluni had picked up a few sentences of English in his time and answered Rattler. 'You use that.'

'That ain't enough,' Rattler scoffed. 'Not fer the amount of whiskey you guzzle.'

'You go get gold. You go Mexico. You buy bullets, whiskey.'

'Where do we get gold?'

'From white eyes' bank. Where else? You dressed like that they no suspect you.'

'Rob a bank? You hear that, boys? OK, Kothluni, we'll give it a try just to show we're friends.'

'You do. You no try to trick us. Or you pay.' Kothluni pulled his thumb across his throat and made a croaking sound.

'We might be able to rob a bank across the border. But we would have to go back to

145

Tombstone to buy whiskey. Unless you want tequila?'

'No, whiskey.'

'Right.' He took a puff of another cigarette that was being passed around and chatted for a while about former members of the band he had known in the old days. Most of them, it seemed had been killed. 'Remember when you took me from the Tucson stage? I always wanted to ask you: what did you do with my mother?'

'Huh!' Kothluni gave his ugly grin. 'The white girl, those other women, we sell them to a man called Creed for firewater.'

'Creed, who's he?'

'Creed. He have one eye, scarface. He buy girls and sell-on down in the town they call Fronteras.'

'Who he sell my mother to?'

'Who know? Maybe to the house where they have squaws for sale.'

'You mean some brothel?'

'I don't know. Bad place. White men are pigs and their women, too. No Apache would do that.'

'A Fronteras brothel?'

'How I know? Maybe Creed keep her for himself. Or sell her to *ranchero* with much money to keep as slave.'

'A rich *haciendado?* I wonder if she's still alive? That must be ten summers ago I last saw her. Ah, well...'

'Why you want to see her?' Kothluni asked. 'No man want her now.'

'She might be still alive, I guess.' Rattler dozed off into a daydream of seeing her again as the Indians chattered. But what would be the use? If alive she would be haggard, ravaged by such a life of sin. She would not want to see him. It was an odd thing about the Apache, they disapproved harshly of sexual infidelity in a squaw. If a woman did have the temerity to stray, the punishment would be to cut off her nose. Quite often as a soldier he had come across a squaw set adrift from the tribe with a bloodily gashed face. To sin with a Hairface the penalty was death. They strongly believed in keeping their race pure. General Crook had tried to wean those on the reservation from this barbaric practice, but it persisted. In some ways Rattler could see their reasoning. They were a proud race. Or had been once.

Back with them Rattler noticed again their odd customs, the wooden back-scratchers that the warriors carried, the kindliness to their children who were never beaten, and he tasted again the sticky jam they ate made from the mesquite fruit, the foul-tasting cactus beer. It looked as if the braves were planning to accompany them part of the way on the raid into Mexico, for they were pushing away those squaws who, as darkness fell, were getting amorous, trying to drag them into the wickiups. The Apache would forswear sex for six days prior to going on the warpath: a warrior believed it sapped his strength. And then, if they stopped for water, they must drink it through a reed so it did not touch their lips. Rattler had never been able to fathom the reason for that. They believed in all manner of gods and spirits who lived in the rocks and trees. They would hunt and kill wild pigs, but never eat them for they knew that the pig was really a devil from the underworld. Yeah, it sure did feel strange being back 'home'!

Ten

Kothluni took the secret trail south through the Guadaloupe mountains which Chirica-hua warriors had used for 400 years or more on their raids into the Spaniards' lands in their quest for horses, scalps, or simply vengeance. There might be a line drawn on the white men's maps called a frontier but it meant nothing to them. He was too canny to go by the easier route, the trail from Tucson south to Nogales, which, now that Geronimo was imprisoned, had become populous again. Trade had resumed, mule wagons going north laden with vegetables and fruit from Sonora, while those heading south carried pig iron and machinery for the mines. The stage lines were flourishing with-out fear of attack and bloodshed, for the route was patrolled by US cavalry and the feared Mexican *Federales*.

The warriors pressed their ponies hard and it took only two days before they came in sight of the town of Fronteras, some way below the so-called border. Kothluni nodded at Johnny Rattler. 'We wait here for you. You come back with gold and bullets. Remember, we hold Seven Clouds and Blue Owl.'

The two Apache scouts looked a little uneasy as Rattler cupped his hand to his hat brim in a casual cavalry salute. The threat to his friends' well-being did not go unnoticed. 'I'll be back. Give me a day or two.'

He jerked his mustang's head around and left the Apaches to lie low in a spur of the mountains as he rode on downriver towards Fronteras. He could see the town's buildings in silhouette against the setting sun as he approached, flat-roofed adobes clustered around – as always in Mexico – the over-sized mission church with its bell-tower. By the time he cantered in, the town had begun to light up for the night.

It was large-sized for a frontier town with *cantinas* and stores doing desultory business in their lethargic, laid-back Mexican way. From an open window came the plangent strains of a guitar playing some slow lament, and from others the clatter of cooking pots, the scent of chilli. Chilli, always chilli, like they wanted to burn their stomachs out!

There were foul-smelling piles of refuse at intervals along the wide sandy street: everything just thrown out, bottles, cans, bones, dirt. But there was something about Mexico that appealed to Johnny Rattler. Why worry, tomorrow you might be dead? So, come on, have a good time!

Johnny paid a dollar in a run-down livery to have his weary mustang hay-fed and given a rub-down, left his saddle in the stall with it and, taking his Spencer carbine, went to inspect the town. Yes, sure enough, they had a bank. 'Banco' the sign said. You couldn't miss it.

He soothed his parched throat with a tequila, a pinch of salt, and a numbing bite of lemon in a *cantina*. Maybe, after all the sweat he had lost, he needed that salt. He leaned on the bar and glanced about him, but there was just the usual humdrum crowd, farm-workers in their baggy pyjama costumes and straw hats, chattering and grinning as the tequila worked its magic ... storekeepers, in more civilized suits, playing backgammon or discussing business as, after the long *siesta* they got ready to open up to trade in the cool of the evening. They posed no threat.

Rattler paid for a rusty-tasting beer and a pile of greasy frijoles and tortillas, hot as hell. He sprawled at a corner table and smoked a ten-centavo cigar. His belly full, he watched the smoke spiral and felt at ease with the world. Maybe he would take a room in the town hotel for the night and leave what he had to do until *mañana?*

But, suddenly, the peace of the *cantina* was shattered. There was the whinnying of spirited horses being hauled in outside, loud shouts or orders snapped out, and a rowdy bunch of men burst into the *cantina*. They swaggered towards the bar, the great rowels of their Mexican spurs clattering as they walked. They wore a uniform of grey with red flashes, short jackets and tight flared trousers. Most sported heavy moustachios beneath their wide-brimmed sombreros, and surly, arrogant expressions. They had the power to do as they pleased with these people and they knew it. The scarlet linings of the capes slung across their shoulders marked them out as the much-dreaded *Federales*.

Rudely they pushed people aside and clamoured for beer and tequila, and took over the centre tables, noisily shoving aside card-players, giving short shrift to any who protested. Not many were foolish enough to do that.

Johnny Rattler knew it might be wise to get up and go, but some stubbornness made him stay and finish his cigar and coffee. He was no darker-skinned than most Mexicans, and in his plaid shirt, cavalry pants and moccasin boots, not unusually dressed in that neck of the woods. Maybe it was the thick Indian hair that cut him out from the rest, or the Colt Frontier stuck in his leather cartridge belt, the Spencer leaning against the wall by his side. Or maybe it was just the lithe, casual way he rocked on the back legs of his chair with an arrogance akin to theirs?

To be sure, the boastful, jeering *Federales* had noticed him, nudging one to the other until all turned to stare. A great fat bear of a man, his uniform patched with sweat, called out, drunkenly, 'Ay-hai, *hombre!* What you doing in here?'

Rattler met his eyes and they clashed with mutual dislike. 'Why shouldn't I be in here?' he asked.

'We don' like Indians stinking up our saloons.'

'I ain't Indian,' Rattler said. 'I'm American.'

'Oh, *Americano*. A *green-go.*' The big man affected a female voice, flapping his hand, limp-wristed, to the merriment of his comrades. 'Just look at the pretty boy's hair.'

'Any law says I have to cut my hair?'

'We are the law,' the big man shouted. 'And what we says goes.'

'Sure,' Rattler said, getting to his feet. 'Waal, nice to meet you folks.'

Surrounded by thirty grinning *Federales* he had decided that discretion might be better than valour and began to ease his way through them. The Spencer in his right hand, he was forced to step over their outstretched legs and, in doing so, one of them brought his foot up hard and sent him sprawling onto the lap of the fat man. Before Rattler could evade him, the bear-hug had him pinioned, and the *vicioso*'s knife was at his throat. 'Not so fast, sweetheart,' he cackled.

Rattler tried to reach for his Frontier but one of the others twisted it from his grip, and another did the same with the Spencer. The big man, twice his weight, had him caught tight and there was nothing he could do about it.

'*El Presidente* Diaz say that we must welcome *Americanos* to our country, but we cannot have them look like this,' the *Federale* chuckled. 'Here, *compañeros*, hold this wriggling fish. I geev him haircut.'

Willing hands pulled Rattler down across a table, cruel faces grinned at him, their foul breath in his face, as the big *Federale* went to work, grabbing handfuls of Rattler's silky black hair and slashing it off until there was just a stubble. One of them fetched a pierglass and shoved it in his face. 'See, is that not better? Now you look like a *man*, not an Apache.'

If they thought to humiliate him, Johnny Rattler gave no sign that he was affected. When they released him, he rubbed his shorn scalp and grinned. 'Waal, boys, you sure saved me the price of a barber. OK, you've had your fun, how about you give me my guns back?'

'*Hijo de puta!*' The big man spat in his face. 'Get out of here before I kill you.'

Johnny Rattler wiped the slime from his

face and stood, proudly, eyeing him. 'Maybe it would be different if it was just you and me. I'd stick you like the pig you are.'

The *Federale* roared like a bear, grabbed Rattler by the throat in an iron grip and back-pedalled him to the door, hurling him out into the dust of the street. He put his boot into the quarter-breed's gut and raked his chest with his vicious rowel. 'You get out of this town, *gringo*, if you know what is good for you.'

Rattler lay and watched the big man waddle back into the *cantina* before picking himself up and examining the bloody spur-tear across his chest. 'Hmm,' he drawled. 'Nice friendly town ... so that's the way they want it?'

He went to sit on a stone bench beneath a willow tree and considered what to do without his trusty Spencer. 'Waal,' he said to nobody in particular, 'at least they didn't rob me. I still got a few dollars left.'

He spied a gun-store and went across. The fussy little man with a celluloid collar welcomed him. Rattler examined his stock. Most of the revolvers were antiques, without doubt more dangerous to the shooter than those shot at. He held them to his ear, clicked the cylinders around, studied the mechanism. Most had the timing of a rusty garden gate. But, yes, there was one, a big old Texas Dragoon that was so solid it would blow anybody's head off at thirty paces. 'You got slugs for this?'

'*Si, señor*, the gun is fifty dollar, the box of bullet ten dollar.'

Rattler loaded the .45 with six from the box, carefully squeezed the rest in the loops of his ammunition belt. He took the last of Sam Cook's crumpled greenbacks from his shirt pocket, counted them out. 'You take American money?'

'*Si, señor*. But thees is only thirty-three dollar.'

Rattler put the barrel of the gun to the little man's forehead and thumbed the hammer back. 'You tryin' to rob me?'

'No, *señor*.'

'Right. I figure thirty-three's enough. You don't want it?'

'Si, *señor*.' The gunshop owner snatched the dollars up.

'*Gracias*. Good to do business.'

Rattler stepped back out into the street, listened to raucous howls of laughter issuing from the *cantina*. They were probably having fun at some poor sap's expense. A few steps down the street was the bank, a hurricane lamp flickering from its barred windows. The revolver swinging from his hand he strode determinedly across. 'Now or never,' he muttered.

'We're closed, mister,' a teller said. He was a young man with wavy hair and was bolting the side of the front doors.

'This says you're still open.' Rattler jabbed the nine-inch barrel into his chest. 'Don't give me trouble. I'm not in the mood for it.'

'Francisco,' the chief cashier called from behind his grille. 'What's the trouble?'

'Me. I'm the trouble.' Rattler kicked the door softly closed and shoved the teller back to the counter. 'Just give me everything you got in the drawer or you both get it.'

'I can't do that.' The cashier, with his slicked back hair and plump well-fed look, stared wide-eyed. 'You wouldn't.'

'Wouldn't I? Try me.' The slug crashed out, shattering the silence, sulphurous smoke curling. 'Start moving that cash across.'

'Oh, no!' the cashier cried. His hand went to his right ear from which blood was pouring. The earlobe was severed. With alacrity he started digging out notes, gold coins, silver pesos, pushing them across. 'Here. Take it. Go. Please, no more shooting, *señor*.'

'Aincha got nothin' to put it in?'

The teller produced a cloth bag and helped him stuff the cash inside. 'Thanks,' Rattler said. 'You may not realize it, but I ain't just doing this for my own benefit, it's on behalf of the US Government.'

'*Si, si.* Now you go.'

'He's robbing the bank,' someone shouted

as Rattler emerged into the street. 'Stop him.'

The *Federales* poured out of the *cantina* opposite him and began blamming revolvers at him as he backed away down the street. 'Hot damn,' he gritted out as he dodged away behind wagons and horse troughs as bullets splintered into woodwork too close for comfort. He crouched down and replied, his shots smashing into the *cantina*'s adobe walls, making the *Federales,* too, seek cover. 'They got me cut off from the hosses. How'm I gonna git outa here?'

Suddenly he saw the big *Federale* come from the *cantina,* the Spencer in his hands and he was levering it with malicious intent. Rattler took careful aim, steadying the Dragoon on a cart-rail. The heavy slug ploughed twisting into the *Federale*'s massive girth, gouting blood. He spiralled like some dainty ballet dancer before toppling into the dust. 'Take that you bastard,' Rattler snarled.

But it was tight papers, that was for sure.

There looked like no way he could get out of there even if he could reach a horse. By now the whole town was roused. In fact, somebody had started clanging the church bell. And Rattler needed to reload.

Ducking low as bullets rattled about him, he raced along the street and dived into an alleyway. He hurriedly tried to reload as he backed away along it, but suddenly he found his back up against a wall. 'Oh, Christ,' he hissed. It was a cul-de-sac.

'Quick!' A female voice spoke from the darkness close to him. A hand reached out and pulled his sleeve. 'Come in here.'

He was drawn, not unwillingly, through a door which was immediately closed and locked. 'Come with me.' The woman led him up a flight of steps towards a landing. He followed her billowing skirts. She hurried along a corridor and entered a room lit by a smoky lamp. 'You'll be safe here.'

'Safe?' He glanced at an old woman lying in a bed, her face the pallid hue of an invalid, her long grey hair spread on the pillow. He could hear a hammering on the door below. 'Can I git out the back window?'

'No. You wouldn't have a chance. Get in with her.'

'In with her?' He gave a strangulated squawk at such an idea. 'Are you joking?'

'Climb in over the other side, hide under the coverlet. Mother, the *Federales* are trying to kill this boy. We must hide him.'

The old woman nodded agitatedly. 'Kill him? Over my dead body.'

'Mebbe that ain't the wisest thing to say,' Rattler muttered as he climbed over her.

There was the thudding of boots, oaths and shouts as the *Federales* hammered on the doors of the rooms in the apartment block. There were screams and protests. Rattler lay with his nose next to the lady's scrawny body under the bedclothes and heard their own door slam open. 'What do you want here, you brutes?' the old woman's daughter was shrieking. 'My mother is dying. How dare you? Outlaw? We have seen no outlaw. A murderer? A *gringo?* A bank robber? So what? What has that to do with us?'

When the *Federales* had gone she hissed, 'Quiet. Don't come out for a bit. You had better stay with us for a while.'

Eleven

'Great Jehosaphat!' Johnny Rattler stared at the silver pesos and high denomination peso notes. 'There's a fortune here they've given me.'

The grey-haired mother looked across from her bed. 'He's won the lottery!'

'Yeah, you could say.' He had tipped the money from the sack onto the floor and was counting it out into piles. 'Jesus! That's about twenty thousand in American dollars.'

'What are you going to do with it?' The woman who had rescued him could not disguise a tinge of awe and envy in her voice. Even a hundred dollars was a lot of malooka in those parts. She was gaunt, dressed in widow's black, her dark hair drawn severely back from a crow-like face. 'I mean, it is much money.'

Rattler smiled askance at her as he counted, licking a finger with his tongue. 'I'm gonna buy whiskey fer the Apache.'

'You *what?*'

'Yeah. It's true.' He looked into her haughty brown eyes. 'And I gotta buy 'em ammunition ... bullets. Could you do a bit of shopping for me before I go?'

'It is you who had better go, young man. We will have no truck with buying whiskey and bullets for the Apache. The next thing you will be telling me it is for that murderer Kothluni.'

'Yeah, too true.' Rattler grinned at her. 'But it's not what you think.'

'Get out.' The woman's face was stern as carved mahogany. 'I don't know what you are up to but I don't like the sound of it.'

'Daughter,' the old woman quavered. 'If he has killed a *Federale* he cannot be so bad. I am glad he has come.'

'They killed my husband in the same way,' the widow said. 'I mean, I thought they were trying to kill you for their fun. I thought you were innocent.'

'He was a fine young man, Felicia. Those drunken brutes tortured and killed him for no reason, just for their sport. Anyone who kills a *Federale* is welcome in my bed.'

'Really?' Rattler was glad to have finally escaped from her bed. She had had a nasty odour about her as he crouched beneath the bedclothes beside her withered buttocks. 'Well, all I can say is thank you, mama.'

'No,' Felicia said. 'You owe us an explanation.'

'OK.' Rattler pushed fingers through his shorn hair and shrugged. 'But when I've told you I'd like you to go across to the gunstore and buy me a hundred rounds of ammunition.'

'For the Apache?'

'*Si*, I've promised to get 'em some. Look' – he reached for her arm, his eyes earnest – 'if I take them these bullets they may kill a few soldiers, perhaps a few innocent settlers. But in the long run it will be their undoing and maybe hundreds of lives will be saved. I'm working with the US Army and we're trying to trap Kothluni.'

'He's a bit of a joker, isn't he?' the old lady cried, trying to sit up against her pillows, her grey hair as wild as a witch's. 'I like him, Felicia.'

'I'm not so sure, Mother. This sounds like some hare-brained figment of his imagination.'

'It probably does, but it's true,' Rattler said. 'I have some sympathy with the Apache. For four years I was brought up among them. But Kothluni – yeuk! He is just a drunken sadist, a bloodthirsty murderer. The day of the Apache is past. It is time this war was over.'

Felicia looked at her ailing mother and shrugged. 'He wants me to go out and buy bullets for the Apache. Have you ever heard the like?' She picked up her faded black *reboso* and wound the shawl around her body and head. 'OK, give me some cash. I will go.'

When she had taken her shopping basket and gone, Rattler said to the old lady, 'These *Federales*, who are they? They seem to think they can lord it over everybody.'

'They are the scum of the earth. Our great father, President Diaz, employs them to grind us down and keep himself in high office. Where do you think he recruits them? In the prisons; murderers, rapists, the lowest of the low. That terrible night they picked on Juan, beat him, whipped him, for no reason. My poor daughter. We could hardly recognize him. That is why we help anybody who is against them.'

'Yuh, I cain't say I took to 'em,' Rattler muttered, and squatted on the floor in thought for a while. '*Madre*, you don't know a fellow called Creed?'

'Creed?' she screeched. 'Yes, I know Creed, or used to. Why?'

'Why? Because I would sure like to know what happened to my own mother. Kothluni said he sold her to him. Mind you, it's a long time ago, maybe eleven summers. I was only eight when they took her from me.'

'Creed,' the old lady murmured. 'Eleven years ago you say? Your mother, was she a blonde, an American woman, blue eyes?'

'Yes.'

'Creed. He was a vile man. He bought and sold women, whiskey, guns, contraband. But, I remember, he took a fancy to that one. He married her.'

'Married her?'

'Yes, he has a *hacienda* and *rancho* out on the Rio Culo de Perro.'

'The Dog's Arse River?'

'*Si*,' she giggled, 'I guess that's how it translates. And it suits him. He's a dog's arse if ever there was one.'

'Is he still there? Is she still with him? How do I get there?'

'How do I know?' the old woman croaked. 'He probably kicked her out years ago. An evil drunkard that man. But you could go take a look. About thirty miles east of here the place lies.'

'Thirty? I could do it in a day. I don't

know why, it's the first time I've really thought about it. But I'd just like to see her. If she's still—'

'I wouldn't put your hopes too high. What with Kothluni and Creed it sounds like you've got your hands full, young fellow. Ah, Daughter!' she cried as Felicia returned with her shopping basket. 'You wouldn't believe it but our young adventurer has set himself another task. He wants to meet Creed.'

'Creed! I would forget that,' Felicia hissed. 'He is a pimp and whoremonger of the worst breed. Here, look, I have got you the bullets you asked for.' She crossed herself, fervently. *'Nombre de Dios!* I only hope I am doing right.'

'You have been very kind.' Rattler could see that without a man to keep them they were living from hand to mouth in this low-class apartment house. 'Here, take this.' He offered Felicia a handful of pesos, about a thousand dollars. 'Take this. Buy yourself a house or something.'

The harsh-looking Felicia pushed the money away, but her mother shrieked out, 'Take it! What does it matter where it came from? The *Federales* owe us that. We can buy ourselves Azul's store. A good clothing business. It is up for sale. We could do well.'

'You seem to have put new life in my mother since being in bed with her,' Felicia smiled. 'Very well, *gracias, señor*. We accept.'

'Oh, we didn't do nothing like that,' the old woman growled. 'Not that I would have objected. He's a handsome young devil, isn't he?'

'Yes.' For the first time a smile broke Felicia's dark wooden mask. 'I suppose he is. Perhaps God brought him to us. Now we must see that he escapes.'

That was easier said than done. A lot of shouting and shooting had been going on down in the street as the *Federales* searched for the bank robber, but gradually it had quietened and they had returned to the *cantina* to brag and drink and discuss their various ideas of where Rattler might be. The *Federale* captain had thrown a ring of men around the town to keep watch in case he was still within the walls and tried to make an escape. Tomorrow they would send out a patrol to seek him. He could not get far.

'Put this on,' the black-haired Felicia said, handing him her *reboso*. It was the Mexican woman's ubiquitous shawl, baby-carrier, shopping bag, nose-wiper and blanket. 'And one of my old skirts. A pity your hair isn't longer.'

'It used to be,' Rattler said, ruffling his coarse crop. 'Until that pig took his knife to me.' He wrapped the long *reboso* around his head and shoulders and stepped into the ankle-length skirt. 'How do I look?'

The old mother tittered. 'Like a pretty *señorita*. You had better beware they don't try to pick you up.'

Rattler pulled the shawl across his face. 'I'll try and make it along to the corral. Thanks again. You saved my life.'

'I hope it was worth saving,' Felicia

smiled. 'Come, I'll let you out.'

Rattler left the cul-de-sac and hurried along the street trying to walk like a girl, the little quick steps they take, and stay in the shadows. Two *Federales* were staggering out of the *cantina* and he ducked his head low as they grinned and shouted at him. He minced on towards the livery on the edge of town where he had left his mustang and saddle.

'Ai-yee! *Muchacha!*' A bandoleer-strung *Federale* suddenly blocked his way. A tubby man in a big sombrero. 'Where you hurrying off to? The night is young. You want some fun?'

'Who me?' Rattler fluttered his lashes at him. He put all his power into the punch, gripping his fist, shooting it out, knocking him flat. 'Out cold! No thanks. Not tonight.'

He pulled one of the bandoleers from the recumbent *Federale*, tossed away his *reboso*, slung the ammunition belt across his own chest, and put on the big sombrero hung with silver conchos. He wound the *Federale*'s scarlet-lined cape around his shoulders and strode into the livery. 'I need the best horse you have,' he said, and tossed the ostler forty silver pesos. 'Saddle it for me, pronto.'

A proud-necked black stallion was brought from a stall and he was assured it was as fleet as the wind. 'Good,' he cried, swinging into the saddle. 'I'm going to look for that damn bank robber. *Adios.*'

As he rode out of town he met a couple of other *Federales* riding the bounds. 'Good men,' he called in Spanish. 'Keep your eyes peeled. Don't let him escape.' He only had to kick his moccasined heels to the stallion and he shot away like a rocket out into the night. Rattler laughed as he hung onto the reins, looking back as the town receded in the moonlight. And then he gave the stallion his head, pounding away, guiding him towards the east. 'Hey! Go there, Diablo!' he cried.

Twelve

The dawn sky glowed like a furnace as Johnny Rattler rode his feisty stallion along the boulderstrewn bend of the river, which was little more than a curving trickle. It was going to be another scorching day. Towards him came a grey-stubbled *peon* riding a donkey, another *burro* jogging along behind him, half-buried by a pile of hay. The *peon*'s woman ran along behind poking the loaded *burro* with a stick to urge it on.

'Animals and females don't have much of a life in Mexico,' Rattler muttered, as he blocked their way, and saw the peasant's fear when he recognized his scarlet cape.

'This hay is from our own patch on the hillside, *señor*,' he whined, kneading his hat in his hands. 'We have not stolen it.'

'Who gives a damn,' Rattler said. 'I'm

looking for the Valle de Suya, a man called Creed.'

'Follow the river through the canyon, *señor*. I beg you, do not tell him you have seen us.'

'Why not, pray?'

'He claims all this land as his. But it has been our right, my father's right before me, to cut hay from the hillside.'

'That why you're out early, huh? What would Creed do if he knew?'

'He would beat me, or even shoot me, *señor*. Please, I beg you say nothing of this.'

'Don't worry, I ain't a snitch.' Rattler touched his sombrero and nudged his stallion on, patting the proud arch of its neck as he stepped high on the uncomfortable rocks. 'Creed don't seem to be very popular in these parts.'

He entered a high-walled canyon which eventually opened out to a wide stretch of grama grass where the river opened up into a small lake, indeed, somewhat the shape of a dog. Amid a grove of willows on one side was an adobe house with castellated walls glowing red in the rising sun's rays. There was a wooden corral and outhouses, a few horses, and scrawny cattle grazing, dotted across the stretch of grass.

Rattler approached cautiously, riding up to the back of the house, tethering the stallion to a branch and stepping silently through the willows. There appeared to be some kind of commotion going on. A flaxen-haired woman tumbled from the door of the house, tripping in the dust in her haste to escape. A tall man in boots, pants and a woollen vest stomped out, a rawhide bullwhip in his hand. He sent it, snaking and cracking, across the woman's bare calves, making her cry out and scramble away.

'Don't tell me there's no milk for my coffee, you stupid bitch. If the cow's gone dry it's your fault.' The man was bald, or shaven-headed, a patch over one eye, and a livid white scar across one side of his face. A frightened peasant girl in a cotton chemise came from the door and Creed, for it must be he, gripped her to him in his muscular left arm. 'Don't come disturbing us again unless you've got some decent breakfast to offer us.'

'Creed, you shouldn't treat me like this. It ain't right.'

'Ain't right?' Creed gave a sneering grin. 'Don't tell me what's right, woman. You're just lucky I haven't kicked your arse outa here. I would sell you, but you ain't worth more than a coupla pesos. You're finished, you *puta*, doncha know that? All you're good for is gettin' my meals. So hurry it up with that milk. Or else.'

As the woman crawled away, climbing upright, Creed cracked the bullwhip to send its lead tip cutting into one of her ankles. He laughed as she screamed, and cracked it whistling after her. 'I want some service in this house.' Creed turned back to the house and shouted gutturally to the girl, who was no more than fifteen, 'Get back inside.'

Rattler peered through the hanging willow

fronds. There did not appear to be any other men on the small ranch. He listened carefully, and his nostrils twitched to the scent of cooking coming from a tumbledown plank hut. He stepped out of cover, glanced at the house, leapt lightly over the shafts of an abandoned wagon, and went over to the hut. It was a poky hole, a stone stove with mesquite coals glowing, iron pots and skillets, a bundle of rags in a corner that served as a bed. The middle-aged woman had her still-shapely leg up on a broken chair and was dabbing at the whip-cuts with a bit of damp rag.

Her once corn-colour, but now greasily flaxen hair hung in a tangle over her face. She wore a ragged skirt and blouse which had slipped over one bronzed shoulder. She suddenly sensed Rattler's presence and turned to him with a gasp of fright. Her face was gaunt, lined by work and worry, the face of a woman in her fifties, but still with the handsome lines that had attracted men to her in her youth. Her blue eyes stared from dark hollows, but were still as vivid as they had always been.

'What do you want?' she cried. 'Who are you? You startled me!'

'Mother.' Rattler felt foolish saying the word after so long. 'It's me.' He took off the sombrero, ruffled his spiky shorn hair and grinned. 'It's been a long time.'

'Johnny?' Her face appeared puzzled, strained, and her lips twisted in a strange grimace. 'Is it really you? How did you find me?'

Rattler shrugged. 'Through the Apache. The one who' – he didn't like to say raped – 'snatched you. Have you lived here all this time since?'

'No. He – did you see that little scene? It is commonplace – you know what he made me do? He worked me in his brothel until I was no longer any good to him, then he brought me here. Men want young girls, not old women. Especially not a woman with a back like this.' She jerked her blouse down and showed him her back knotted with hideously interweaving scars. 'See that?'

'He did this?' He touched her, delicately, with his fingers. 'Why do you stay with him?'

'What else can I do? Where go? Who would have me?'

'Why didn't you ever try to find me?'

'I was convinced the Apache had killed you. Anyway, what would have been the use? What happened to you?'

'I was brought up by Kothluni for a bit and then by the army. It's a long story'

'So, what are you now, a *Federale?*'

'No, I killed one yesterday. I robbed a bank. I'm heading back across the border, if I can.'

'So, you don't waste your time! What do you want here?'

'What do you think? I wanted to see you.'

'So, now you've seen me. Go.'

'Come with me.'

'What? I cannot come with you.'

'But you can't stay with him, like this?'

'Why not? I have got used to it. He is a

lazy drunken brute, it's true. He beats me, flaunts his concubines in front of me. He will be in bed with the poor girl now. He treats me as his skivvy. But he is my husband' – she showed him a gold ring on her gnarled finger – 'how can I leave him?'

Rattler studied her, sucking in his cheeks, thoughtfully. 'I can't take you now, anyway. I have to go back to the hills to Kothluni. The lives of two of my friends depend on it. But I can come back for you.'

'Forget it. You sound like you're in enough trouble already. You don't want your old mother along.'

Rattler went to look out of the door as Creed came from the front door of the house and roared, 'Amanda! Where are you? You don't bring that coffee and milk over here in five minutes you'll be in trouble. I'm warning–'

Suddenly he spotted the slimly built youth standing in the doorway of the hut in the shadows. 'Who the hell are you?' he roared. 'What do you want here?'

'For a start,' Rattler shouted as he stepped forward, 'I want you to treat my mother with a little more civility.'

'Your mother?'

'Yes, if you ever lay your whip on her again' – he pointed an outstretched finger at Creed – 'you will have me to deal with.'

His mother had run out and caught hold of his arm. 'Don't, please. Don't cause trouble, he will kill you,' she hissed. 'He is just going, Creed,' she said. She had always called her husband by his surname, as all others did. 'This is Johnny, my son. I haven't seen him since the Apaches got us. He just wanted to see me. He is going now.'

'He sure is. So this is that lousy 'breed? Johnny, eh? Well, you just listen to me. That bitch of a woman's my wife and I'll treat her just the way I feel. If you ain't off my property in sixty seconds you'll regret it, boy. And don't you ever come back poking your dirty nose in where it ain't wanted. You savvy?'

'And you, Creed, I've told you' – Rattler

pointed his finger at him again – 'you ever touch her with that whip and it will be the last thing you do.'

'Yeah?' Creed howled, tensing it in his hand. 'Maybe you'd like a taste of it, too? She's gonna get the biggest beating of her life for this. I'm going inside, boy, and when I come out in a minute's time you'd better be gone, 'cause I'm goin' to have both barrels smoking.'

'Go!' His mother screamed. 'For God's sake, leave.'

Rattler pushed her aside and stepped closer to the house across the yard, loosening the long-barrelled Texas Dragoon. He bit his lip: it wasn't his customary kind of handgun, too heavy. But a raw anger made him determined to stand his ground. 'Come on then, Creed,' he called.

'No, Johnny!' his mother shrieked.

The bald-headed man burst from the open house door, a scowl on his scarred face, one good eye glimmering. He had a double-barrelled sawn-off twelve gauge in his hands and he had thumbed both hammers. 'You're askin' fer it, son.'

The first barrel's blast ripped through the air above his head as Rattler knelt, holding the Dragoon in a double grip to steady it. The Mexican girl had run out, clad only in a sheet, catching hold of Creed's arm, and, unintentionally, jerking the shotgun up. Her action undoubtedly saved Rattler, but he hesitated to fire for fear of hitting her. Creed threw her off and aimed from the hip again.

Rattler rolled aside across the dust to avoid the hissing buckshot scatter and aimed the Dragoon propped up on his forearms. Creed hurled the spent shotgun at him and went for his own revolver, but, as he did so, Rattler's heavy slug tore through his jugular. Creed spun to one side, his legs and arms flailing to keep his balance. *Boom!* Rattler squeezed the trigger again and his second shot crashed into Creed's back. He got to his feet, but Creed was still not dead, blood gouting from his body as he attempted to crawl away. Rattler emptied the revolver into him.

When Creed was finally still he turned to his mother and said, 'There's one varmint who ain't gonna bother you no more.'

'What have you done? Oh, God!' She ran and knelt beside the dead man, rolled him over. 'He was my husband.'

'He ain't no more. Good riddance I'd uv thought you'd say.'

'You don't understand.' She stared up at him, her blue eyes filling with tears. 'We been together a long time. What am I going to do now?'

'Maybe you could cook *me* some break-fast?' Rattler blew down his smoking barrel and began to reload from his belt. 'I ain't so fussy about cream in my coffee. Come on, Ma' – he went and patted her shoulder – 'you're free of him. You can do whatever you like from now on.'

He looked up at the girl draped in her sheet. 'You better git dressed and go back to where you belong.' He spread his hands to them as they gaped at him. 'Fer Christ's sake, it was self-defence. He tried to kill me. Remember you tell that to the lawman.'

Killing a snake like Creed did not bother him overmuch. It certainly did not spoil his breakfast when his mother brought it to him in the house. In fact, he'd got quite an appetite. 'I dunno what he was complainin' about,' he said, sipping the black coffee. 'This is good.'

His mother sat on the edge of the crumpled bed and watched him. 'I'm glad he didn't kill you,' she smiled. 'You've grown up to be quite a man.'

'It looks like you'll inherit this place if you're really his wife.'

'I don't know. It's mortgaged to the hilt. All he's probably left me are gambling debts. The place is falling to rack and ruin. He ran a whorehouse in town but that, too, wasn't doing so well. It was the drink ruined him. That's why he went around like a bear with a sore head.'

Rattler had brought the stallion round to

the front of the house and given him some grain. He had brought the bank sack in with him. He tipped the contents on the bed. 'I'll be needing some of this, but you take half.' He put a hand between the notes, silver and gold coins. 'That's about ten thousand dollars. Enough to pay your debts and settle the mortgage on this place.'

She took the money, wonderingly. 'I don't know ... this is stolen cash.'

'So what? So is most everybody's. Tell 'em you found it in Creed's safe. Come on, take it, everything will work out. You deserve a break.'

'I'm not sure of this, Johnny.' She smiled for the first time that day, reached out and smoothed his cheek. 'Will you come and stay here? We're well off the beaten track. Folks will soon forget about those things you've done. There isn't much law in these parts.'

'I don't know. I got things to do first. Anyway' – he stood and stroked her hair – 'I gotta be going. It's been good seeing you.

I'm sorry about your man, but he did kinda ask fer it.'

'Don't be sorry. I'm getting used to it. Once he's buried he'll be gone. I do believe I'm glad.'

Thirteen

Diablo, the stallion, was as powerful as Amigo had been, but with brutish nature. He took every opportunity to bite, or kick, or throw his unsuspecting rider. He had been treated badly in his time. No wonder the ostler had been quick to get rid of him. Johnny Rattler managed to control him using the cruel spade bit, but he would have preferred to do it by the tone of his voice, the pressure of his knees, by gaining the horse's confidence. The ornate Spanish harness included a martingale to hold his head arched downwards. Maybe he was a stargazer, maybe not. Maybe they just liked to torment the poor creature. To prevent any ideas he might get when he was in harness about mounting some mare or other, he had a curious contraption girding his loins, vicious spikes that quickly deterred his male part from becoming erect. A kind of male chastity belt that knocked any such ideas out of his head. But one thing was for sure, he was fast. Almost as fast as Amigo.

Johnny Rattler had taken the chance of traversing north of Fronteras to head back into the mountains again. But the *Federales* were looking for him and when he ran into a patrol they gave whoops of glee and began firing immediately as they charged after him. Rattler gave Diablo his head, hanging low over his neck, the black mane flying in his face, bullets zipping and whining about him as he quirted the stallion from side to side. On and on he pounded across the plain, gradually drawing away from the patrol. He rode straight as an arrow, kicking up a cloud of dust, until he saw the canyon where Kothluni had said he would wait. He veered away into it and his pursuers gave more shrill yells for they thought they had him trapped. How wrong could they be? They rode straight into the ambush, arrows hissing out to thud into chests, carbine bullets knocking them from their mustangs before they had time to reply. The Apaches showed themselves, leaping down from the rocks and onto the backs of the startled *Federales*. The sergeant in command drew his revolver, firing rapidly at the savages, but Kothluni's lance took him out. When they saw their leader on the ground, the Apache chief calmly removing his scalp, those left on their horses gulped with fear, turned and raced away as fast as they could back to Fronteras.

'The cowards!' Rattler jeered.

It was a grisly sight, the jubilant Apaches hacking hair from the fallen *Federales*, roping the wounded to cactus and ant piles to give them the slow death.

'So!' Kothluni said. 'You have come back.' He pulled his lance from the sergeant's back. 'You have brought us scalps. You have had good hunting?'

'You got plenty of ammo now,' Rattler said, tossing his saddle-bags to him. He pulled a handful of cash from his pocket. 'I got enough yellow stone here to buy you a whole wagonload of whiskey. I had to kill two white eyes.'

'You take no scalps?'

'Well, the last one was as bald as a billiard ball so there weren't much point,' Rattler grinned. 'The man Creed. I have had vengeance.'

'Good. You have done well. You are a true warrior.' Kothluni gave his evil toothy smile. 'What has happened to your hair?'

'The bastards caught me, cut it off. They thought they could take my power. But they did not succeed.' He touched the snake rattle on its cord around his neck and shouted to the other warriors. 'This is my power. Your great chief Kothluni gave it to me when I was a boy. While I wear this I cannot fail.'

The warriors gave howls of approval and went back to their butchering. Kothluni called them off. They left a few of the former desperadoes pegged out in the sun to die horribly and trailed away. 'We go back to the San Carlos,' Kothluni shouted, the bloody scalp swinging from his lance. 'Rattler will buy us whiskey.'

Johnny grinned at Blue Owl and Jack Seven Clouds, who had managed to take little part in the massacre. 'If you ask me he's a damn drunk!'

'We're taking the wagon out to the reservation, dear,' Mrs Holm said. 'It's such a lovely day. Do you want to come along for the ride?'

'You're not doing deals with Agent Tiffany again?' Pearl cried. 'You'll be getting yourself into trouble one of these days.'

'Pah!' Josiah Holm, a thin, reedy little man, armed himself with his shotgun. 'It's damn good beef. Too good for them savages. Anyway, there's hardly any of them left. The bucks been shipped off to Fort Pickens, Pensacoola and a good job, too.'

'Are you sure it's safe, dear?' Her mother had similar features to Pearl, but hers were

196

wreathed in a padding of comfortable fat. She put on her shawl and tied her best bonnet. 'Isn't Kothluni still at large?'

'No, he's been chased by the cavalry south of the frontier. He was sighted down near Fronteras causing mayhem. He won't venture back this way in a hurry. At last we can look forward to peaceful trading.'

'If you don't want to come you stay and look after the store, Pearl.'

'No, I'll come,' the girl said. 'It would be nice to get out from this place. I don't get much chance of a ride these days.' And her cheek dimpled mischievously as she thought of Rattler, wondering where he had got to.

It was, indeed, pleasant to go jogging along on the empty wagon, sat up on the driving seat beside her parents, watching the swinging tails of the double-harnessed team, and, as they left Globe, and the great gashes of the copper mines, and climbed steadily up to the San Carlos, to see the bleak and rocky desert of the reservation land spreading out before them.

'There it is,' Trader Holm said, flicking his long whip towards the log-built agency building in the distance. He pulled out his watch. 'Nearly noon. We're spot on time.'

In the past he would have gone out on his own under cover of darkness to do his shady deals with Tiffany. But now he felt confident there was little danger. It made a pleasant outing for his family.

'There he is,' Mrs Holm cooed, and fluttered her fingers as she saw the gaunt figure in his black frock coat and Quaker hat standing outside the agency talking to two Indian guards. 'Hello, Mr Tiffany.'

Tiffany looked surprised to see the females, but touched his hatbrim. Facially he was not unlike the former President Lincoln, a prow of a nose, hollow cheeks, sharp gimlet eyes, and a collar of black beard above his white shirt and loose bow. 'Waal,' he drawled. 'Pleased to meetcha, Miz Holm. This, I take it, is that purty young daughter of yours. My, she's growed into a real woman.'

Pearl tossed back her blonde curls, and gave a sniff of her dainty nose. She had never much cared for the crafty-looking agent. Nor his carryings-on, the way he cheated his charges. 'I'll be sixteen next month, so I guess I *am* a woman,' she said.

'You come fer the goods?' Tiffany growled at Holm. 'I got sacks of flour and sides of beef fresh in. You better come inside. You, boys,' he called to the guards, 'give us a hand.'

Pearl jumped down and watched as the men lurched out with the heavy sacks and muslin-covered beef and loaded it onto the back of the wagon. Her father greedily rubbed his hands as he fussed about the loading. He was going to make a fine profit. When the goods were tarpaulin-covered he went over to the store doorway and she saw him counting out greenbacks into Tiffany's hands.

'Good to do business with you, Trader Holm,' the agent said as he came out to see them off. 'Goodbye, ladies.'

199

'What a lovely day,' Mrs Holm cried. 'It's so nice to know we're at peace, at last.'

'Yes, the days of trouble are over.' Tiffany grinned wolfishly at the girl. 'Maybe I'll call on you when next I'm in town.'

'Do. I'm sure Pearl would love to see you.' As Holm began to manoeuvre the horses around, the mother whispered, 'He's a senator's nephew, you know.'

'Yes,' the girl said, unimpressed. 'I suppose that's how he got this job.' As she stared at Tiffany her mouth fell open with shock. 'Oh, my God!'

An arrow had hissed past her head and entered Tiffany's throat, emerging from the other side spouting blood. The agent gave a strangled cry and fell back in the dust. Pearl looked around and saw naked Apaches, their bodies camouflaged with mud and leaves wriggling silently as snakes through the rocks and cactus towards them. The Apache guards, in their black hats and dark uniform coats, ran to grab up their carbines leaned against a rock. A warrior burst from the undergrowth his bow strung taut. *Tzit!*' The arrow sped to embed in the first guard's abdomen as he raised his gun. The second guard levered his Winchester and shot the warrior down, backing away towards the agency building, firing the repeating carbine. But more warriors raced from the rocks, cutting him down with bullets and arrows. They gave whoops of triumph as they began to hack at the three men's bodies, fighting for trophies.

'Yaaagh!' Mr Holm lashed out at the cart-horses with his whip, sending them plunging forward. His wife shrieked with fear as she hung onto his arm. Pearl gritted her teeth and gripped the side of the wagon as they went lumbering away down the trail with the heavy load. 'Faster!' she cried.

Diablo pricked up his ears when he heard the gunshots. Johnny Rattler glanced at Kothluni, on his mustang by his side. He had sent the advance party of ten warriors in to scout the agency. They had no orders to attack. As one, they kicked their horses forward, followed by the rest of the Apaches, and charged towards the agency building. A wagon pulled by two horses was rattling and careering down the trail. A white man was lashing them with his whip as two females clung to the box. Several of the warriors jumped onto the trail and hauled the frightened horses to a halt.

'Jeez!' Rattler gasped to Jack Seven Clouds. 'It's Pearl.'

Trader Holm had seized a shotgun and fired at one of the warriors hanging onto the horses. The Apache fell to the dust peppered with bloody holes. Kothluni rode up, taking the shotgun from Holm as if disarming a child. He tossed it aside and plunged his lance into the little man's chest.

Rattler had half a mind to try to seize Pearl and make a run for it, but he was surrounded by thirty-five grinning warriors, some of whom had already got their hands on the two women and were pulling them down.

Mrs Holm was screaming in a frenzy of

fear as she was dragged by the hair to one side and two of the savages began tearing her clothes off.

Pearl was frozen with fear as she, too, was dragged in the dust and it became apparent what the Apaches were planning to do with her. Her eyes suddenly met Rattler's with an agonized plea. 'Johnny! Help me!'

Rattler swung from the stallion and hauled the warriors from her, cracking one across the jaw with his revolver butt, kicking another away. He jumped back, kneeling over her, gripping her dress front in his left fist, spinning the Dragoon to clutch the walnut grip and turn it on the ring of curious warriors. They surrounded him, watching, their weapons poised, waiting for Kothluni's command.

'She is mine!' Rattler shouted in their language. 'A moon ago I took her. She is my squaw.'

He knew he didn't have a chance if they attacked, but he was prepared to die fighting for her.

Kothluni stared, his eyes unfathomable, stroking his chin. He prodded the girl with his bloody lance tip, prodded her pale breasts, revealed by the torn dress, and grinned. 'You his woman?'

Pearl gulped and nodded. 'Yes, he is my man.'

'Kothluni, you owe me,' Rattler hissed. 'I've helped you. Spare her.'

'OK, we don't kill pretty girl,' Kothluni grinned. 'You have her. But, first, you go get me whiskey. I keep her here safe.'

'No, let me take her with me.'

'Kothluni has spoken.' He probed harder with the lance so she flinched. 'You go. Bring much whiskey. She yours.'

'You give your word?'

'I am Kothluni.' He proudly tapped his chest. 'I no lie.'

'What about this one?' a warrior called. He was squatted over the hysterical Mrs Holm, her ample curves exposed. 'She for us?'

Kothluni shrugged and turned away. 'You have.'

The mother gave a piercing scream as the warriors fought to grab hold of her, as if she was the prize in a tug-of-war. Kothluni reached out and took the girl's arm. 'You come with me.' He led her back towards the agency building.

'There's nothing I can do.' Rattler gave Pearl a drink from his canteen as she sat in the shade. She looked dazed and stunned. Kothluni had gone inside to inspect the place. But his six warriors stood watching, guarding her. 'You gotta try and hang on. I'll be back with his whiskey in a coupla days, I hope. Then, with any luck, he'll let us go.'

'What are they doing to Mother?' She gave a shudder as she spoke the words. 'Will they kill her? Can't you help her?'

'No. I'm sorry. I can't. They have to have one of you. I'm lucky he's agreed to hand you over. Pearl, you gotta be strong. For us. We're gonna get through this.' He stroked a hand gently across her damp brow, stroking the hair into place. 'I better go soon.' He buttoned her torn dress. 'You're the one I want, Pearl. You know that.'

'Yes, Johnny,' she whispered, hoarsely, her lips trembling, 'but, I'm so frightened.' Tears began trickling down her cheeks as she started sobbing.

'Hold on, Pearl.' He gripped her arm. 'They're gonna take you up to Hell Canyon. I'm gonna meet 'em there. Wait for me.'

There was a sudden piercing shriek from down the trail. Rattler jumped up, and went to take a look. Mrs Holm was not a pretty sight. He padded back to the girl and shook his head, grimly. 'I'm sorry, Pearl. She's gone. They killed her.'

Kothluni was loading the beef and flour up onto the cart-horses and mustangs, leaving what they could not carry for who-soever wanted it. Some of the reservation Indian women and children had arrived to watch, curiously, hungrily, as Kothluni put the building to the flames.

Rattler swung onto Diablo as the warriors began to trail away. He glanced at the slaughtered Tiffany and Holm. 'Well,' he muttered, 'they kinda got what they asked for.'

Pearl was pulled to her feet, her hands roped in front of her and tied by a loose lead to Kothluni's saddle. She would have to walk across the rough ground ... or run. She met Rattler's eyes, pleadingly, as she was dragged away.

He whirled Diablo around and set off for Globe. He put the stallion to a hard lope and when he reached the small mining town cantered in down the curving street. It was mid-afternoon and the town was quiet, not many people about. He hoped nobody would recognize him in his new plaid shirt and with his hair shorn short. He jumped down at the telegraph office and dictated a message to Captain Hentig at Fort Bowie. MEET ME SOONEST AT ROSITA'S CANTINA TOMBSTONE STOP COME INCOGNITO STOP EAGLE.

As the old guy began to tap out his message he dashed out and onto Diablo, giving him a cut from his wrist-quirt, racing away down the main street and out onto the trail through the mountains to Tombstone.

'Hey,' the town barber said, as he sat whittling in his rocker outside his shop. 'Wasn't that that kid Rattler they're looking for?'

Fourteen

'Well, I'll be gol-darned!' Captain Hentig exclaimed as he read the telegraph. 'It sounds like it might be time to make our move. Loo-tenant Prendergast, get a platoon of our crack sharp-shooters ready. We're heading for Tombstone.'

Hentig carefully shaved before a small mirror in the back room to his office that served as his quarters, scraping the cut-throat across his neck with the unthinking practised ease of a man who had done so most mornings of his life even when out on the trail. He liked to look neat. He splashed his cheeks in a tin bowl and tossed the water out of a window. He pulled on his faded combat jacket, his yellow bandanna, knotting it loosely, and selected a Win-chester carbine from the rack.

'Bring that stallion Amigo around,' he shouted to Sgt McMullan, who had bustled into the office. 'Have him saddled for me. Every man to carry fifty rounds and hard-tack rations for six days.'

Hentig buckled on his gunbelt and, as was his wont before going out on a mission that might prove dangerous or fatal, glanced around at the contents of his room with its Indian curios of Sioux, Cheyenne, Comanche and Apache hung on the adobe walls, the souvenirs of his campaign; the much-thumbed set of Shakespeare. That summer he had re-read the three great tragedies, *Macbeth, Caesar* and *Lear*. There was a calico sheet draped across the ceiling to catch scorpions and tarantulas and stop them dropping on his head, a cot with its woven blanket, a small chest of drawers with the framed likenesses of his mother, his father, his sister and ... Maureen. It wasn't a lot to show for thirty years.

'Platoon!' he shouted as he mounted up and raised a white-gloved hand. 'Forward.'

He led them at a jogtrot out of the fort, the mountain peaks a hazy blue in the late afternoon.

The sun bled away like molten gold on the horizon as Johnny Rattler cantered into Tombstone, its rays silhouetting the clapboard false-fronts. From the hundred saloons came the sound of music and laughter as miners, gamblers, cowboys, drifters and the flotsam of Arizona caroused. He hauled Diablo in by the blacksmith's corral when he saw Tribollet's fancy-painted wagon abandoned in the yard.

'I come to collect my father's wagon,' he said. 'You got a couple of stout hosses to sell to put in the shafts?'

'Ain't I seen you afore?' the smithy asked, wiping his hands on his leather apron. 'If he was your father you must be that young Sergeant Rattler who escaped custody.'

'Thass right. But I'd be obliged if you don't mention it to anybody,' Rattler smiled.

'I'm kinda undercover.'

'It ain't none of my business. I'm jest here to attend to hosses. Surprised to see you still alive, thassall.'

'Yeah? Sometimes I am, too. Can you give my stallion a feed and a washdown? I'll pay you now. I might be in a hurry later on.'

'Yeah, I guess you might. Waal, I s'pose you're legally entitled to the wagon, though I thought it was in military custody.'

'Nah, they won't be needin' it now. I'm settin' up in business for myself.'

'I'll believe ya,' the blacksmith drawled, taking Diablo into his barn. 'This is some feisty brute. I'll have two good wagon-hosses waitin' for ya.' As Rattler counted out cash, he protested, 'No, thass too much. You'll be needing change.'

'You keep it,' the youth said. 'With my thanks.'

It was dusk by now and he sauntered away into the narrow streets of the old Mexican quarter lit by hurricane lamps or whale oil flares. He parted the bead doorway of

Rosita's Cantina and his face lit up when he saw Conchita dancing in the centre of the floor to a strumming guitar. The ruffled skirt of the girl's dress whirled like a toreador's cape as she spun on her slim bronzed legs, clacking her high heels and snapping her fingers, swaying sinuously,. She froze like a statue when she caught sight of Johnny, only pausing to pick up the coins that men tossed onto the floor for her.

'Aiyaa! *Querido mio!*' she shrieked, darting across to catch hold of his arm. 'You come back to me.'

'Sure, how are you, you minx?' He grinned as she wound her wiry arms around him and rained kisses on his cheeks. 'I ain't just here to see you. I'm on business.'

'Minx? What is this minx?'

'It's a compliment.' He lurched forward to the bar with her still attached to him and called for a bottle of tequila. 'I'm here to meet a pal of mine. A tall feller, gittin on a bit, clean-shaven, you know, has an Irish way of talkin'.'

'Ire-rish. What is zis Ire-rish?'

'Aw, you know, he's American but talks with a kinda lilt.' Rattler spat the bottle cork away and poured them two tumblers full. He bit into a portion of lemon, winced, took a lick of salt, and tossed the spirit back. 'You seen him?'

'No. I no see him. This bar for Mexican people.'

'Yeah, so I see. A real low-life dive, ain't it?' He glanced around at the men sprawled on benches drinking, others at crude wooden tables playing games of chance. Most were packing iron and draped with belts of ammunition, wearing big sombreros, leathers and velveteens. He was glad he had taken the precaution of hiding his cash away, the notes tucked in his boots and hat-band, the coins mostly stashed in his saddle-bags. It wouldn't do to let these ruffians know the sizeable amount he was packing. Nor Conchita, neither. He could feel the prostitute's expert fingers exploring his trouser and shirt pockets as she hugged and kissed him. 'Hey, hang on,' he said, snatching back a roll of pesos she had come up with in her hand. 'You can't have all that. I need to buy a few bottles of whiskey.'

'Come on, Johnny,' she wheedled. 'You know you wan' me. How much you geev me?'

'You jest hold your hosses. We got all night to celebrate.'

Captain Hentig and his dozen picked troopers made camp in a canyon on the outskirts of Tombstone. As night fell he changed into the spare 'civvy' clothes he had packed, a crumpled grey homespun suit, grey wool shirt and loose bow, replacing his cavalry hat with a low-crowned Stetson.

'Jesus, Mary and Joseph!' Sgt McMullan exclaimed as he stepped into the firelight. 'I didn't recognize you, sor. Have I got the date wrong? Is it you already retired?'

'Ach, don't fuss yourself, Sergeant. I got another two days to go in this man's army. You could say I'm jest gettin' into the way of t'ings. I'm takin' a ride into town to meet a young friend of mine for a chin-wag.'

'Shall we ride along with you, sor?'

'No. I don't need a nursemaid.' Hentig buckled on his gun beneath his coat. 'This is all on the q.t., you understand? We don't want folks to get wind of any military goings-on. There ain't many Apaches left on the loose but they still got spies around.'

'This is highly irregular, sir,' young Prendergast put in. 'Do you want us to dress down, so to speak?'

'Nope. I should be back before dawn. Just be ready to ride.'

Prendergast watched the captain climb up onto Amigo. 'Good luck, sir.'

'We may be needin' some before this outing's over.' Hentig casually saluted, and spurred out into the night. 'Be seein' ya,' he called.

Sheriff Perry Owens was sitting in his leather chair with his boots up on his desk reading the weekly newspaper when the town mayor poked his head in. 'I just heard a whisper,' he hissed. 'Rattler's in town. He was seen going into the Mex quarter. Do you want me to raise a posse of guns?'

Owens stared woodenly at his newspaper. 'No, I don't, Mr Mayor. Don't go gittin' in a lather. Rattler ain't no big deal. I can handle him.'

The roly-poly mayor removed his derby and mopped at his brow with a spotted 'kerchief. 'But he's a dangerous renegade. We ought to–'

'We didn't oughta do nuthin'. Just don't speak a word of this to anybody.'

'We don't want any more innocent blood shed. If there're any more slayings in this town it's your job that's on the line, Owens.'

The sheriff put his feet down and stood to face the mayor, flicking back his long hair over his shoulders. 'Mister Mayor, I want you to just shuddup and go home. I'm keeping the lid on this town and I know what's going on. Rattler's working for us, you understand? Just say nuthin' to nobody.

Or' – he spun one of the revolvers on a finger and aimed it at the mayor's portly belly – 'it'll be you who's out of a job.'

Captain Hentig parted the bead curtain and peered inside the smoky *cantina* before ducking his head and stepping through. A villainous crowd if ever he saw one. They ceased their chatter and gave him a surly once over. Non-Latinos were not particularly welcomed in this joint. Many had ended up with a scarlet necktie and been dragged away down the back alley.

'Howdy, gents,' he drawled, and stepped over to the bar. 'Don't s'pose you stock whiskey, d'ye?'

The chubby Mex bar-owner was washing some mugs and drying them on his apron. 'You know, you're the second man to ask that tonight.'

'You don't say? Would he have been wearin' a kinda rattlesnake tail on a cord around his throat?'

'He might. What's that to you?'

'I'm a friend. He asked me to meet him here.'

The owner eyed him. 'Yeah, he said about you. A tall gringo.' He jerked his head. 'He's out back with Conchita.'

'Yeah, I mighta guessed.'

'Hiya, Cap.' Rattler appeared from a side door in the act of buckling his belt. 'Nice to see ya.'

'Some dive you've invited me to. Couldn't you have picked a classier place?'

'This OK. These guys they don't split on nobody. So, what you drinking?'

'I got what you want,' the barman said. 'You want see?' he beckoned Rattler into a back room and opened up a crate, pulling out a bottle of red-eye whiskey. 'Good stuff.'

'Fine.' Rattler pulled out some notes and paid him the agreed price. 'Let's give it a try.' He went back in the bar, pulling the cork with his strong white teeth. 'This should put hair on your chest, Cap.'

'Maybe you should use less of the Cap. You can call me George.'

'Aw, I couldn't do that. It don't sound right.'

Conchita reeled into the bar looking a tad drunk, either on love, or tequila. 'Ah, you got me another customer.' She squeezed in between them, tossing her dark curls, her eyes dull as sloes, looking up slyly at Hentig, running catlike claws over his shirt.

'Beat it.' Rattler pushed her roughly aside. 'My pal ain't int'rested. We got things to talk about. Go bother somebody else.'

'You lousy 'breed,' she snarled, turning on him a volley of Spanish oaths. 'You can't treat me like this. I am Conchita. Remember? I feex you. I feex you good.' She looked about ready to stick a knife in his side.

'Aw, come on, honey. Give us a break. I'll see you some other time.'

'Ach!' she yelled, turning away. 'Anybody with *greengo* blood they theenk themselves too good for us. We feex them, eh?'

'Quite the little fire-cracker,' Hentig said. 'Where you find 'em, boy?' He took a nip of the red-eye and all but spat it out. 'What the hell you call this stuff?'

'Ssh,' Rattler said, lowering his voice, dragging him over to a corner seat. 'It ain't for us. It's for you-know-who, the Big K. He's been raidin' and killin' again up at the San Carlos. I don't know if you heard yet? He snatched a girl, my girl. Killed her folks. He reckons he'll exchange her if I take him a wagonload of whiskey. This stuff. I got the wagon ready down at the corral.'

'Good.' Hentig considered the situation. 'What we waitin' for, Rattler? Let's get the damn wagon loaded and hit the trail. You can tell me the rest as we drive.'

'Cap, I need to get Pearl out safe. You give me your word...?'

As they slipped out of the *cantina* they heard a voice snap out, 'Hold it right there. Raise your hands.' The barrels of twin revolvers dug into their backs. 'OK, turn around slowly. You try anythang, you're dead.'

They turned and looked into the pale eyes of the sheriff, Perry Owens. He peered at them in the half-light from the *cantina*. 'George? What the hell you doin' here?'

Captain Hentig beckoned him away from the bar. 'We're going after Kothluni. You coming?'

'That's army business.' Owens thrust out his chest like a bantam rooster. He twirled the twin Frontier revolvers and adeptly returned them to their holster. 'I don't think I will. I got taxes to collect, this town to keep an eye on. I jest wanna know what's going on, thassall.'

As they parted, Hentig growled to Rattler, 'I never thought Owens would turn yeller.'

'No, nor me,' the youth said.

Fifteen

Hell Canyon was a narrow defile through one thousand foot high walls of rock, deep in the fastnesses of the mountains. In secret caves above, the Apache had their hide-outs which had proved almost impregnable. Kothluni, in his scarlet headgear, perched on a rock and watched the horses pulling Tribollet's travelling wagon slowly approaching across the desert in the mid-morning heat. His hawk-eyes studied a smoke sign drifting into the air six miles away. 'He is alone,' it announced. Two warriors came riding up on their ponies, leaving them at the foot of the cliff, to bound up the rocks to him to confirm this news. There was no sign of any troopers – the long knives – following, or anywhere in their land.

'He brings the whiskey,' he grunted. 'Good.'

Kothluni sprang down to a lower cave outside which their few squaws and children were gathered about a cooking fire. He peered inside the dark entrance and saw the pale-skinned white girl. Her wrists were bound with rawhide and her blouse and skirt were dusty and torn from travelling, but she had not been otherwise hurt. 'You keep her here,' he said to the women. Then he shouted to the thirty or so warriors, the last guardians of their land, 'Come!' They went racing down behind him to leap onto their painted ponies and jogged away along the sandy canyon. They were, as always, armed and ready for war.

Johnny Rattler sat on the box and urged the tired horses onwards, sending a rawhide whip whistling over their backs. The painted wagon, with its wooden sides that could be let down to form gaming tables – Tribollet's travelling casino – rattled along and entered the deep shadow of the high walls at the entrance to the canyon. He had hitched his former chestnut stallion, Amigo, behind, and beside him on the box was an open crate of bottles of hooch.

'How much longer I got to sit here?' Sgt McMullan groaned from behind him. 'I got cramp in me backside.'

'Quiet,' Rattler said. 'Here they come.'

He reined in; grabbed a bottle and waved it as the Apaches came from the canyon and rode towards him. 'I got you a load of best red-eye,' he shouted to Kothluni, and threw him a bottle. 'Where's the girl?'

The wizened chief caught the bottle, pulled the cork, took a swig and grinned toothily. 'When the whiskey is ours you get the girl.'

'Here.' Rattler began tossing more bottles to the warriors as they gathered around the wagon. 'Help yourselves.'

They gave screaming whoops of glee and began prancing their mustangs around the wagon as they tipped the firewater down their throats. But Kothluni was, as always, suspicious. It was why he had stayed alive so long. 'Open the back,' he commanded.

'Sure.' Rattler jumped down on the sand, drawing his knife, and stood as if to cut the ropes tying the canvas doorway. Instead, he slashed Amigo's hitching rope and leapt into the saddle, screaming, 'Now!' He swung the stallion around and raced away.

The wooden sides of the wagon rattled down and sixteen troopers were revealed, six on each side and two at the front and the back, including Captain Hentig and Lt Prendergast. 'Fire!' Hentig yelled and his own Winchester barked out to topple the first warrior in his sights.

The volley of lead roared flame and leaden death, decimating the surprised warriors. Some managed to hurl their lances or raise their carbines to reply, but most were immediately cut down. Some tried to wheel their mustangs away, but the experienced troopers took careful aim, potting them like ducks on a pond. However, they did not have it all their own way. A Corporal

Wiggings collapsed, instantly dead as a bullet pierced his brain. And Captain Hentig gasped and fell back as a lance thudded into his side.

Meanwhile, Rattler had ridden away in a half-circle, pulled his carbine from the boot and was causing havoc to those Apache who tried to make a break. Kothluni had given a scream of rage and started to chase after him, but when Rattler's bullet nearly took off his scalp he changed his mind and returned to the battle. It was his lance that floored Hentig.

Kothluni looked around him at his warriors dead and dying. It was a bad day. He cursed himself for not suspecting a trick. He gave another scream of anger, turned his mustang and raced back into the dark canyon. He was intent on escape, but first he would take vengeance on the white squaw.

Rattler saw him go and kicked his heels into Amigo setting off in pursuit. Kothluni had a good start on him, but as he charged up the shadowy canyon Amigo's speed began to tell. Kothluni, however, was still a short way ahead when he leaped from the mustang and darted away up through the rocks of the lower cliff. Rattler raised his carbine and fired, but as Kothluni jumped to one side, he missed. He tried again, but there was only a dull click. He had spent his seven. He tossed the carbine away, jumped down and set off after Kothluni.

It was a hard climb to the lower cliff, but, his lungs bursting, Rattler scrambled after him. He knew what Kothluni was planning. Gradually he caught up with the old warrior chief. He threw himself forward and grabbed hold of his moccasin boot, hauling him back. Kothluni twisted around, swinging his tomahawk, a scowl of hatred on his face.

'Traitor,' he screamed. 'You betray The People.'

Rattler ducked the blow that whistled past his cheek. He caught hold of Kothluni's arm and wrestled him for the weapon. At one

228

point their faces were almost touching as the muscles of their arms bulged in a test of strength.

'I promised whiskey,' Rattler gasped out. 'You got it. That was the deal.' Kothluni, with his free hand, had managed to pick up a rock. With a howl of rage he smashed it into Rattler's face.

The youth went slithering down the slope, blood running from his cheek and, when he looked up, dazed, he saw Kothluni reach the cave from which women and children were hastily running away. Kothluni went inside and came out dragging Pearl by her hair. The warrior raised a knife in triumph about to plunge it into her neck.

'No!' he heard Pearl beg.

There was little Rattler could do in his dazed state. He lay there and watched in horror. Suddenly a revolver shot rang out, and Kothluni slowly dropped the knife and reeled back to the cave wall. He was still dragging the girl, trying to use her to protect himself. Rattler saw the long-haired Perry

Owens jump down from behind a rock and approach the cave mouth, firing his Frontiers double-handed. Kothluni writhed in agony before finally crumbling. He gave a long drawn-out cry, 'Aaaagh!'

Rattler picked himself up and joined Owens by the prostrate warrior. 'The last of the fighting Apache,' the sheriff said, blowing down the barrels of his revolvers. 'At least, let's hope so.'

'Pearl.' Rattler squeezed the girl in his arms. 'Are you OK?'

'Yes,' she murmured, clinging to him. 'I think so.'

'Where the hell did you come from?' he asked Owens.

'Where you think? I followed along taking cover. You didn't think I was going to miss the action, did ya?' He grinned at Rattler. 'OK, you varmint. Thass enough kissin' and cuddlin'. Git your hands up. You're under arrest.'

'No,' Pearl protested. 'That's not fair. He saved my life.'

'No, I did that, sweetheart,' Owens said. 'Come on, let's git back to the others.'

They found the troopers well in control, only a few cowed and wounded renegades left alive. Jack Seven Clouds had been killed in the action. Blue Owl had survived by turning his gun on his own kind. 'How's the Cap?' Rattler asked.

'Not so good.' Lt Prendergast shook his head. 'He's losing a lot of blood.'

Rattler jumped up onto the wagon and found Hentig lying on his back still clutching hold of the lance in his side. 'Here, Cap, we gotta git that out.' Rattler wrenched the lance free. 'Anybody got a canteen?' He washed the gaping wound then poured whiskey over it. Hentig gasped with pain, perspiration bursting from his brow. 'Holy Mary, Mother of God! Who woulda thought it? I was to be retired tomorrow.'

'You're gonna be OK, Cap,' Rattler said, plugging the wound. 'I think it's missed your vitals. They gotta git you back to Tombstone soon as possible. Can you hold on?'

'I dunno, Johnny. How about you? What's happened to your face?'

'Aw, that's nothin'. Lie still, Cap. We'll git you back.'

'Rattler,' Hentig gripped his wrist. 'I ain't sure General Miles will honour his word about reinstating you. You better git outa here while you got the chance.'

'I ain't got the chance.' Rattler looked at Owens, who was standing at the wagon gate, one Frontier still in his fist. 'He's taking me in.'

'Aw.' Owens spun the revolver back into the holster. 'Who are you? I fergit. Go on. Skat! And try not to cause them *Federales* too much trouble.'

Rattler smiled at them. 'So long, Cap. Give my love to Maureen.

'I will. Take Amigo,' the captain whispered. 'Ride free, Johnny. Ride free.'

Rattler jumped from the wagon, swung up onto the chestnut. 'You coming, Pearl?' He put out a hand and swung the girl up behind him. 'How about you Blue Owl? I'm real sorry about Jack.'

'No. I go back see Ekinata. I make her my squaw. I hope we live at peace now.'

'I have to admit I was wrong about you, Sergeant,' Lt Prendergast said to Rattler. 'May I congratulate you? You have proved yourself to be a fine scout. You not only led us to Kothluni, but you saved this girl's life, too.'

'Thanks, Lootenant,' Rattler grinned. 'You ain't such a bad guy, yourself, after all. Why don't you take one of them scalps? Something to show your folks back East. You won't get another chance.'

He waved to them and shouted, '*Adios, amigos* – you, too, McMullan,' as he set off at a fast lope into Hell Canyon planning to wend his way through the border mountains. 'I think you're gonna like my mother's ranch,' he called back.

Pearl squeezed her arms around his waist and hung on tight, her face pressing his shoulder. 'I know I am, Johnny,' she cried.

The publishers hope that this book has given you enjoyable reading. Large Print Books are especially designed to be as easy to see and hold as possible. If you wish a complete list of our books please ask at your local library or write directly to:

Dales Large Print Books
Magna House, Long Preston,
Skipton, North Yorkshire.
BD23 4ND

This Large Print Book for the partially sighted, who cannot read normal print, is published under the auspices of

THE ULVERSCROFT FOUNDATION

Other DALES Titles
In Large Print

JANIE BOLITHO
Wound For Wound

BEN BRIDGES
Gunsmoke Is Grey

PETER CHAMBERS
A Miniature Murder Mystery

CHRISTOPHER CORAM
Murder Beneath The Trees

SONIA DEANE
The Affair Of Doctor Rutland

GILLIAN LINSCOTT
Crown Witness

PHILIP McCUTCHAN
The Bright Red Business